BUSHWHACKER'S GUN

BUSHWHACKER'S GUN

•

CLIFFORD BLAIR

AVALON BOOKS
THOMAS BOUREGY AND COMPANY, INC.
401 LAFAYETTE STREET
NEW YORK, NEW YORK 10003

PRINTED IN THE UNITED STATES OF AMERICA
ON ACID-FREE PAPER
BY HADDON CRAFTSMEN, SCRANTON, PENNSYLVANIA

To the victims, their
families, the rescue
workers, and all those
touched by the bombing
of the Murrah Building,
Oklahoma City, April 19, 1995;
Oklahoma stood proud . . .

Prologue

When the ragged, buckskinned figure appeared on the ledge eight feet above the trail, Glen Douglas had already canted his Winchester across his saddle to bring it to bear on the apparition. "Howdy, Quirt," he drawled.

The newcomer's gaunt, bristled face split to bare gnarled yellow teeth in what might've been either a grin or a snarl. The narrowed eyes flicked to the rifle. "You heard me coming, did you?" he husked.

"Something like that."

The arrogant tilt of Quirt's head, and the way his hands fondled the big Sharps buffalo gun he toted, told Glen that he'd only heard the other's approach because Quirt had wanted it that way. He wasn't surprised. When it came to stalking skills and stealth, Quirt

1

might've been bold brother to the Apache warriors of old. With the afternoon sun behind him, Quirt's shadow lay dark across the trail.

"What are you doing haunting these mountains, Quirt?" Glen asked coldly.

The grinning snarl widened. "Likely the same thing you're doing."

Glen raised his left hand to thumb-flick the silver badge pinned to his shirt. "I'm doing lawman's work."

Quirt gave a snort as he nodded. "It's like I said, we're both on the manhunter's trail."

"The difference is, I'm a Deputy U.S. Marshal."

"And I'm a bounty hunter, same as you been one time and another."

"There's a difference between hunting a man for a bounty, and killing him for it."

Quirt sneered. "Not in the eyes of the law. Dead or alive, the money's just the same."

Beneath Glen his horse shifted, and he tilted his head to keep his gaze on Quirt. In addition to his greasy buckskins, the renegade bounty hunter was clad the same as he'd always been when Glen had crossed his trail in the past. Apache moccasins, a tattered gunbelt where sheathed bowie and holstered six-gun hung side by side, and a shapeless Stetson with his long tangled hair falling from beneath it gave him almost the look of an old-time mountain man. The image was made even stronger by the big .50-caliber Sharps.

Quirt hefted the long-barreled rifle now. His grin was evil. ''All I ask is, let me get some wanted varmint in the sights of my bushwhacker's gun here, and the bounty on his sorry head is all mine.''

Quirt was boasting, but what he said was pretty near the unvarnished truth, Glen knew. The loner's reputation for ruthless accuracy over long distances with his rifle was a byword among the law enforcers and the lawbreakers alike in the Indian Lands where he prowled.

Glen, like now, did some prowling there himself. With the partial opening for settlement of Oklahoma Territory to the east, these lawless Indian Lands had become a last bastion for the owlhoots, bandits, wide-loopers, gunslicks, and other renegades who for years had run free in what was now Oklahoma. Opposed only by the ineffective efforts of the displaced Indian tribes, which had been forcibly settled there, and whatever local law could be mounted by the scattered towns in the area, the lawless breed had held undisputed sway hereabouts. The Lands provided hideouts for outlaws on the run from their depredations in the more civilized surrounding areas, as well as sanctuary for wanted men of every ilk from all over the nation.

Faced with a violent no-man's-land in the very heart of its growing country, the U.S. government had appointed one man, and given him all but free rein to deal with the problem. That man was Judge Isaac

Charles Parker—the Hanging Judge, as he was known by folk on both sides of the law.

The moniker wasn't misplaced. Parker had realized early on that only a man as ruthless as the outlaws themselves had any chance of corraling them and bringing peace to the Lands.

From his courthouse at Fort Smith, Arkansas, Judge Parker sent his deputies out with few restrictions on their use of force. Those outlaws who were brought in alive more often than not met their Maker at the end of a hemp rope on the order of Judge Parker himself.

Parker's deputies, among whom Glen was numbered, were as hard-bitten a bunch of fighting men as ever pinned on a tin star in the violent history of the West. Outnumbered and outgunned, they opposed the lawless rabble in a hundred different gun battles and showdowns, and, gradually, the tide had turned in their favor.

Though still a region where many men lived by the gun out of choice or necessity, the Indian Lands had become a safer place for the hardy homesteaders who negotiated with the tribes for the right to settle there.

But the Lands weren't fully tamed yet. They still bred loners like Quirt who trod the boundary of the law. These low, rugged mountains were a fitting realm for him. The remote fastness of the forested limestone peaks had long been a sanctuary for hunted men. The twisted maze of canyons, caves, cliffs, and pine woods made tracking human quarry a risky business, especially when that quarry might be looking to turn the tables on the hunter.

"You got business with me, Quirt?" Glen growled. The trail he followed would be growing cold if he let the bounty man delay him much longer.

"Just wanted to let you know I was here," Quirt answered easily. "Didn't want you throwing down on me by mistake, thinking I was some low-life outlaw."

"I wouldn't throw down on you by mistake," Glen told him deliberately.

Quirt hitched his shoulders. "I reckon not," he said and chuckled with a sound like gravel shaking in a bucket. "You up here after the same bunch I am?"

"Just passing through."

Grinning, Quirt shook his head. "Naw, not a law hound of your breed. You can't fool me like that; you know who I'm meaning. Them four backshooters who cleaned out the bank over in Stillwater after gunning down a teller and a customer. I figure you're sniffing their scent just like I am."

"Don't get in my way, Quirt."

"Wouldn't think of it. But I would give some thought to you and me joining up to go after them four yahoos. You cotton to that?"

"Reckon I'll pass."

"What for? Nothing wrong with reducing the odds a little. You and me would make a good team. And I wouldn't say that about just every hombre coming down the pike."

"Thanks," Glen said dryly. "But it sounds to me like you're just looking for someone to share the risks, and not the rewards. Deputies don't get bounties; you know that." He shook his head. "Guess I'll turn you down on your offer."

Quirt's ugly grin became more of a snarl. "You're missing a good bet."

Glen shrugged. "Could be." He loosened his fingers on the Winchester; he'd been gripping it too tightly.

"Suit yourself, Deputy." Abruptly Quirt's shadow disappeared. He vanished like a wraith among the rugged boulders behind him.

Glen swallowed. He was glad Quirt wasn't stalking *him* through these mountains.

He jigged his horse forward, keeping his attention divided between the sign he followed and the surrounding terrain. Other dangers besides Quirt might lurk hereabouts. The faint tracks were fresh.

From beyond a massive hogback ahead of him, a horse whickered.

Glen yanked up sharply enough on the reins to keep his own mount from answering. Quickly he dismounted and, leading his horse into concealment behind a towering pillar of stone, left it tied and muzzled. He stayed off the trail, moving on foot through the rugged terrain of upthrusting ridges of rock, yawning crevices, and sheer stone walls.

Cautiously he ascended the hogback, hampered by

his rifle, but unwilling to discard it. He crested the
ridge on his belly, and felt his teeth grind hard together
with satisfaction. His prey was loafing about the canyon floor below.

As yet, the quartet hadn't done much about seeing
to their horses or making camp. They appeared more
interested in joking and passing around a bottle. A
sagging lean-to and the blackened circle of a dead fire
indicated they had holed up in this spot before.

Only a burly, bearded jasper Glen took to be the
leader seemed concerned about pursuit. He didn't join
in the laughter, and frequently he cast his eyes search-
ingly up at the surrounding peaks. All of them were
packing handguns. Their rifles, if any, had been left
on their horses farther down the canyon. It had been
one of the beasts that had betrayed their presence.

Glen ran a practiced eye over the grade below him.
It offered plenty of cover for a man who knew his
business.

Quirt had been right, he reflected. The odds were
heavy. He was one man looking to corral four. But it
wouldn't be the first time. The trick was in being close
enough to get a dead drop, so that none of them dared
buck him.

He gave it a few moments longer to be sure there
were no lookouts. Then, warily, he began to work his
way down the slope. He stayed to cover, using the
terrain, the scrub brush, and even the lengthening
shadows for concealment. The bearded leader had

grown a bit less watchful, and cast only occasional glances about.

Up close to their camp, flat on his stomach, Glen doffed his Stetson and peered cautiously over a sheltering boulder. They were a hard crew, right enough, he assessed; no strangers to powdersmoke and life on the dodge. Running guns to a man, he mused sourly. And just the sort of pickings Quirt would be drawn to. The bank in Stillwater had offered a reward—five hundred dollars apiece for their capture, dead or alive.

They were clustered together now, seated in a companionable circle and still passing the bottle. Snatches of their crude conversation and coarse laughter reached Glen's ears clearly. None of them, he gauged, were expecting trouble.

He gathered himself, limbering his muscles. Hard experience had taught him that, if he threw down on them from cover, there was no way to guess how they'd react. Likely he'd have to drop at least one of them, and some lead would be thrown his way, before he convinced them the threat was real. He hadn't lied to Quirt. He had no wish to gun down any man—even an owlhoot—if he could sidestep it. Better to let them see him right up front.

He drew a deep breath and let it out. Then, straightening to his feet, he stepped into the open, Winchester at the ready.

"Grow roots, boys," he growled and jacked a shell into the chamber for emphasis. "Sit tight and don't move a muscle."

Two of them were seated so they were facing him, and the sight of the rifle stopped their convulsive grabs for their six-guns. The other two had to crank their heads around to get a look at him.

"Nice and easy, and everybody lives," Glen said flatly. "Now, stand up and keep your hands in sight. All of you face me."

They obeyed. As he'd counted on, their bemusement at his unexpected appearance and calm coolness had kept them from trying anything.

For the moment. But the danger wasn't over yet.

"Shuck your guns, one at a time." He held the rifle centered so he could swing it to bear on any of them who showed fight. He gave a nod to the bearded leader on his left. "You first."

Carefully, his eyes aflame, the chieftain made to comply. Just as his hand touched his gun, there came an ugly thwack of impact, and the outlaw on Glen's right gave a startled grunt and began to fall.

Glen was reacting even as the yahoo's knees buckled. He didn't need to wait for the faint, far-off boom of the Sharps to know what was happening. The outlaw chieftain guessed it too. Shock, then rage, twisted his face almost simultaneously. His fingers clamped about the butt of his pistol, and he started his draw. Glen triggered the Winchester and shot him in the middle. He folded, his gun—only half-drawn—dropping back into his holster.

Just a hair slower, his two other compadres were

hauling iron. Glen dropped to one knee as his right hand flicked down, then up, working the lever to jack another shell into the Winchester's breech. He swung the barrel in line with the owlhoot next to the collapsing leader and fired again. Out of the edge of his vision he saw the final outlaw jolted backward by some unseen force.

All four owlhoots hit the ground within almost the same second. The distant roar of the final shot came echoing down out of the mountains to reach Glen's ears.

Reflexively he levered the Winchester again, but there was no need for any further shooting. Four men had been rendered dead or dying in maybe not that many seconds.

Glen looked up at the rugged rocky faces looming above him. A puff of powdersmoke, made tiny by distance, hung above an outcropping of boulders. A good six hundred yards, Glen estimated bitterly. He resisted the savage impulse to drive a futile rifle shot up at the betraying smoke. The bullet from the Winchester wouldn't have hit anything.

He tensed his legs and rose, conscious of an uneasy prickling at the back of his neck. If the bushwhacker hadn't been accurate, or if he'd wanted him dead along with the outlaws, Glen knew he'd be sprawled there beside them.

A seething molten heat rose up in him as he examined the bodies. He tamped it down as he knelt beside the fallen chieftain.

After a moment he rose and walked carefully to a convenient boulder. He set the Winchester aside in plain view and propped himself against the boulder, half leaning and half sitting. Arms crossed over his chest, he waited.

Slow minutes plodded past. This time he heard no betraying sound, although he sensed the scrutiny of piercing eyes.

"Coming in, Deputy," the familiar voice sang out.

Glen cocked his head and didn't answer.

"Told you we'd make a good team," Quirt said through his brazen grin as he appeared from out of the rocks.

The big Sharps dangled from his right hand with seeming carelessness, but Glen saw that it was cocked and no doubt ready to be swung into thundering action. Quirt was still playing it careful, but Glen's discarded Winchester, and his arms crossed well clear of his six-gun, had made the bounty hunter relax his guard a mite.

Glen let him amble to within a handful of yards before he spoke. "I ought to haul you in and charge you with murder," he said tonelessly.

Quirt's eyes narrowed. "For throwing down on this scum?" he jeered. "You know they're all wanted. Alive or dead, it don't matter."

"Then maybe the charge should be interfering with an officer of the law."

"Why, Deputy, I was just doing you an unasked

favor and giving you some cover when I saw one of them yahoos make his play. I might've saved your life. Face it, law hound, nobody'd listen to you. Even the Hanging Judge would laugh you out of court.''

''Could be,'' Glen conceded.

Quirt nodded with satisfaction. ''Now you're talking sense.''

''So maybe I ought to just drill you right now.'' Casually Glen brought the outlaw chieftain's gun out from under his arm where he'd held it concealed, and leveled it at Quirt's chest.

Quirt froze like a deer that had just scented a cougar.

''I told you not to get in my way,'' Glen said quietly. He kept an eye on the cocked Sharps in case Quirt tried to tilt it up and fire it one-handed.

But the bounty man stayed still. ''Now simmer down,'' he suggested. ''There's no call for this.''

''Don't cross me again, Quirt.'' Glen bit the words out like pieces of ice. ''Not ever. You savvy?''

Quirt's eyes held a feral savagery, but he nodded as though his neck was made of hardwood. ''I get your drift.''

''You better. Now lower the hammer on that blamed cannon.''

Deftly Quirt complied. Glen eased down the hammer on the purloined Colt and let the barrel sag.

Quirt drew a shaky breath of relief. ''What about them?'' he jerked his head toward the four bodies.

"Take them."

Quirt blinked in surprise. "You ain't pulling my leg?"

Glen shrugged negligently. "I got no use for them."

Quirt's grin was almost amiable. "That's more like it, Deputy. I'm mighty obliged to you. By rights, two of them's yours." He turned eagerly toward the fallen owlhoots.

Glen watched him without expression. He had no intention of letting Quirt collect blood money on his victims. He'd reach a town with a telegraph line long before Quirt could haul his grisly burdens back to Fort Smith. A telegram to Judge Parker would scotch any hopes Quirt had of getting paid for this day's bloody work. Glen sighed wearily. His small measure of retribution didn't make him feel much better.

He abandoned Quirt to his grim task and went back to his horse. He kept an eye cocked over his shoulder as he rode out, but saw no signs that Quirt was looking to even the score.

He shook his head tiredly. He'd had his bellyful of this ugly business, he thought suddenly. All he'd done in trying to bring the outlaws to justice was to set them up as easy victims for a bounty hunter's gun. Disgustedly he tossed the bandit leader's pistol aside.

It was time he got himself shed of this sorry trade too, he reflected sourly. He'd saved up some of his earnings. He could use the funds to get into a line of work with a better future.

He would put his manhunting days behind him.

Chapter One

When he saw the circling buzzards, Glen Douglas had a dark notion of what he was going to find. He felt his face draw taut as he put heels to the ribs of his pinto and headed toward the scavengers at an easy lope under the late summer sun. Likely not much need for hurry now.

He pulled the pinto up as he drew closer. His hunch had been on the money. His horse shuffled and snorted uneasily at the smell of death. Glen held him steady. Even mounted, he could see all he needed. He sighed bleakly with recognition.

A heavy-caliber bullet fired from a long ways off had done the job. The victim had probably been on his way to or from town along the pair of ruts that served as a road here on the prairie. His horse had

14

bolted when its rider had been dumped from the saddle by the impact of the drygulcher's bullet.

How many did this make? Glen questioned silently. Five for certain; six, if you counted the first fellow from early in the summer. But he'd been dead a spell, and nobody knew for certain who he'd been. But they had all died like this man, alone on the plains almost under the shadow of the towering Arbuckle Mountains.

Glen glanced up at the uneven outline of the small mountain range. The outermost hills were no more than a half mile back from the road. He ran his eyes over the scarred limestone face of the nearest peak and tried to quell the grim auspicions that had come to him of late.

All six of the victims had been killed in like manner—shot at long range by a marksman who seemed to favor the cover of the rugged slopes and draws of the Arbuckles. All of them had been local farmers or ranchers, neighbors of Glen, men he had known.

He knew this one too. Jacob Parmiter had run a few head of scrawny cattle and raised enough in the way of crops to get by from year to year. Glen remembered him as an easygoing, taciturn man with a nondescript wife who had mothered a trio of stairstep children. He seemed to recall talk of her having family back East. Maybe they could take her and her young ones in now that Parmiter was gone.

Glen dismounted and went through the motions of

checking for life. He doubted Parmiter had ever known what hit him.

Shaking his head regretfully, he straightened to his feet and cast his eyes once more toward the mountains. For an instant red ants seemed to crawl on his nape as he fancied himself in the sights of some unseen rifleman.

He scowled and shrugged the eerie sensation from him. Parmiter's body should be taken into town, he figured, and he would need another horse to get the job done. The Turner place was the closest hereabouts. He could go there and borrow an extra animal.

Mounting, he wheeled the pinto and left the still form behind him. His face grim, he cut across country at a gallop. He had been on his way into town himself. If he'd come along a little sooner, would he be the one lying sprawled there on the prairie?

He slowed the pinto to cross one of the rare railroad lines that had penetrated the Indian Lands. The horse's shod hooves clattered over the rails. With the coming of the trains, Glen could foresee the approaching doom of what was left of the tribes. Now that the rails had brought white men and their scattered settlements into the vast grasslands, the demand would grow for the lush territory to be fully opened for homesteading. Other parts of what had once been Indian Territory had already been opened to the east. As matters stood now, the tribes had some say-so over who came to live in these parts. It wouldn't stay that way forever, Glen predicted.

He rode through a scattering of grazing cattle bearing the Bar T brand of the Turner spread. A mixed lot, he noted with an expert's eye. But even at their worst, these hardy range cattle were a cut above the longhorns of the old days when it came to producing beef.

Cresting a grassy ridge, he drew rein to study the Turner homeplace below him. The house was a sturdy, functional structure. The barn and the small corral attached to it looked to be in good repair. Glen gave a faint nod of approval. The boy was doing a fine job, he reflected.

Old Isaiah Turner, a widower, had been the dry-gulcher's second sure victim a couple of months back. Since that time, Pete Turner, his teenage son, had done his best to make a go of the spread. Glen had stopped by regularly to give him a hand, but hadn't set foot on the place in several days. He was pleased with what he saw.

He jigged the pinto down the slope. Halfway down, he noted a surprising splash of color in one of the front windows. It was, he saw, a spray of late-blooming wildflowers in a simple earthen vase. It seemed a little out of character for young Pete, he thought with a frown.

As he pulled up in front of the house, Ranger, their hound, came from under the porch and let out a couple of desultory bays.

''Hello the house!'' Glen called when the pooch had quieted. The front door was open in the afternoon heat.

A curtain moved, and he sensed eyes on him. He waited, and after a moment there was a flurry of movement and a pretty young woman in a blue homespun dress stepped through the doorway, eyeing him cautiously.

Glen blinked. She made a fetching picture standing there on the porch, dust rag in hand, with the afternoon sunlight glinting from her blond hair.

He had no idea who she was.

She'd obviously been caught in the middle of some household chore. Her hair was done up in a tidy fashion to keep it out of her way while she worked, but a few stray strands had come loose and now framed her face becomingly. She was tall and had a figure that filled out the dress in a way Glen liked.

Her right arm was held straight down by her side, her hand out of sight in a fold of her dress. He caught a familiar gleam of metal and realized that she was holding a hogleg of some sort in that hand. No helpless schoolmarm this, he mused with a touch of respect. But her presence certainly explained the flowers in the window.

''Yes?'' she inquired in a puzzled tone that carried an edge of caution.

Glen became conscious of the fact he'd been gaping at her like some moonstruck yokel. He shut his mouth, then found his voice and opened it again. ''Howdy, ma'am. I'm needing to borrow a horse.''

Her puzzlement showed on her pretty features.

"You've got a horse," she pointed out. Her right arm tensed a bit. "Who are you?"

"Name's Glen Douglas," he managed, then added, "I own a spread over to the north a ways."

Her expression softened. "Oh, Peter's mentioned your name. You've helped him out since . . . since Dad died." She blanched slightly.

"You're Pete's sister?" Glen inquired.

She gave a quick nod. "I'm Barbara Turner. I came back home to give Peter a hand now that Dad's gone."

Glen recollected some talk of Isaiah having a daughter who was staying with kinfolk up in Kansas until he and his son had made a go of things here in the Lands. The vague memory hadn't prepared him for this lovely young woman still plainly touched by grief over her father's passing.

"Pleased to meet you, Miss Barbara," he offered belatedly.

"Just Barbara, please. After all, we're neighbors. And, heavens, I'm forgetting my manners. Step down, won't you? Peter should be back shortly. He rode over to check on some of the stock." She made to motion with her right hand, then flushed prettily as though just remembering the gun she was holding.

Glen hesitated, then dismounted to give her a moment to get over her discomfiture.

"You must be thirsty," she asserted. "I've got some tea made."

"Obliged."

Still looking flustered about the gun, she turned to disappear into the house. Glen stood awkwardly, holding the pinto's reins and waiting for her return. The dog crawled back under the porch. Glen realized he'd almost forgotten his purpose in coming here.

She reappeared minutes later with two mugs of tea. The gun and the dustrag had vanished. Glen noted she had taken the time to tuck in the few straying strands of her blond hair.

He stepped forward to meet her as she came down off the porch and extended one of the mugs toward him. He wondered if it was only his fancy that her fingertips brushed his as he accepted the drink. He sipped the tea, watching her over the rim of his mug. Cool and sweet, the liquid felt good to his parched throat.

"I've just been out here for a couple of days," she explained, tasting her tea. "I haven't had time to meet all of our neighbors yet. Peter had been so busy with the crops and the herd that he let a lot of things go here around the homeplace. I've been cleaning the house today." She touched a hand reflectively to her hair. "I'm certainly not a fit sight for company."

"You look mighty fitting from my view," Glen said honestly.

Her cheeks colored, but she accepted the compliment with a pleased smile and a little quizzical tilt of her head. "Peter didn't say anything about you being able to turn a girl's head with talk like that."

Glen felt blood rise to his own face. The remark had come to his lips unbidden. He'd never been much of a man for the ladies. He took a big sip of the tea and remembered enough in the way of manners not to smack his lips in appreciation. He thought he detected sparkles of amusement dancing in her brown eyes.

"Anything Pete needs a hand with?" he asked to get on safer ground.

"Nothing he and I can't handle," she assured him then broke off and pressed her even white teeth into her full lower lip. The sparkles disappeared from her eyes.

"You and Pete having troubles?" Glen asked immediately.

She frowned prettily. "Not real trouble, I don't believe." She seemed reluctant to share problems with a virtual stranger.

"Something's sure fretting you," Glen prodded gently.

She squared her trim shoulders as though reaching a sudden decision. "I'm sure you know Jason Rathers," she said.

Glen nodded, wondering where this was headed. "He has the biggest spread around here. Was one of the first white men in this area. He leased a lot of land from the Indians, and has kept adding to it when he could. Word is, he can be a rough customer when he gets riled."

She nodded as he spoke. "Well, shortly after Dad

was killed, before I could come out here, Rathers made an offer to Peter to buy us out.''

''Not even Rathers can buy land here,'' Glen objected. ''It all belongs to the Chickasaws.''

''No, not the land,'' she corrected quickly. ''Just our cattle and all this: lock, stock, and barrel.'' She gestured about at the house and outbuildings.

''I reckon Pete turned him down,'' Glen opined.

She nodded firm assent. ''Peter told him he wasn't interested. Rathers left it alone till I arrived, then made another offer to both of us. It was a fair price too.''

''But you still said no.''

Another quick nod of assent. ''Rathers got kind of ugly then,'' she went on. ''He said we were taking on too big of a load, and that he couldn't be responsible for what happened to a couple of kids trying to run a ranch.'' She gave a little defiant lift to her chin, and Glen could tell the contemptuous description of her and her brother had rankled.

Glen frowned. ''Have you heard anything more from him?''

''No, and I really don't know why I mentioned it at all. I'm sure he was just upset that we wouldn't take him up on his offer.''

Glen shrugged. ''If you need a hand with Rathers or anything else, give me a shout.''

She smiled her gratitude, and Glen was suddenly aware of the heat from the afternoon sun on the back of his neck.

Uncomfortably he drained the last of his tea and handed the mug back to her. "Thanks." This time he was sure their fingers brushed. Her eyes dropped quickly away from his. "I best be moseying on," he said. "If I could trouble you for the loan of a horse, I'll have him back to you this evening, or in the morning, first thing."

"Oh, that's right," she said with evident chagrin. "I'd forgotten all about you wanting a horse. But what ever do you need one for?"

Tersely Glen explained, regretting the need to do so. He watched as her face grew pale. Once more she pressed her teeth into her lower lip, and he knew she was again feeling the loss of her pa. He resisted the sudden urge to reach out and draw her comfortingly to him.

"These killings are so terrible," she moaned softly. "Who could be doing them?"

Glen didn't answer.

"And the law can't do anything about it," she went on. "We asked Oscar Manning, the town marshal in Davis, to go after Dad's killer, but he refused. Said his jurisdiction stopped at the edge of town. Actually, I think he was just scared that if he went after the killer, he'd be the next victim."

Glen didn't give her an answer. This was the sort of job tailor-made for the Deputy U.S. Marshals. But the ranks of the deputies were thinning these days, what with veterans like himself retiring to put down some roots, the gradual advance of civilization, and the slow establishment of law and order in the Lands.

"I better see to getting that horse," Glen said aloud.

"Of course." She collected herself quickly. "Peter's riding the gelding, but our mare and the mule are in the pasture behind the barn. Take the mare. The mule gets balky sometimes.

Glen nodded his thanks. "Tell Pete I said howdy."

She stood watching as he stepped into the stirrup. He fancied he felt her eyes on him until he disappeared from her view on the far side of the barn.

He found the roan mare at the far end of the small pasture and had little trouble dropping a loop on her. He was leading her back toward the gate when the drum of approaching hoofbeats made him pull the pinto up sharply.

A handful of riders appeared over a neighboring hill and headed toward the house at a gallop. Glen squinted, and his face tightened into a scowl. "Speak of the devil himself," he muttered.

He'd only set eyes on him a couple of times, but he reckoned as how the gent leading that pack was none other than ranch owner Jason Rathers.

Chapter Two

Glen loosened the rope and flicked it from the neck of the mare. She snorted with disdain and trotted triumphantly away. Glen edged the pinto into the shadow of the barn beside the fence of the corral. The riders were just pounding up to the house to be greeted by the challenging bays of the hound. From the look of things, they hadn't noticed Glen's presence in the small pasture.

He dismounted and slid his Winchester from its sheat. Leaving the pinto standing, he eased to the corner of the barn where he could command a view of the house and the newcomers now reined up in front of it. Something in the aggressive way these yahoos had ridden in, coming on the heels of Barbara's remarks about their boss, raised the hackles on Glen's neck.

25

They weren't cowhands, he saw immediately. Armed to the teeth, carrying themselves with wary bravado, they had all the earmarks of a crew of fighting men. Hard cases and gunslicks, they were of the same breed he'd come to know all too well during the seasons he had spent behind a badge.

The ramrod siding Rathers looked to be the most formidable of the bunch. Tall, and powerful through the shoulders, he kept his hand close to his holstered gun with a natural ease that came only from years or riding the gun trail. Beneath his flat-crowned hat, Glen glimpsed a rough-hewn face seared to a leathery brown by long exposure to the unforgiving elements. Glen guessed his eyes would have the same manhunter's squint he himself saw sometimes in the mirror.

''Anybody home?'' the tall graying man at the front of the pack called out as if he owned the place.

Glen put his gaze on Jason Rathers. The ranch owner sat his horse with an arrogance born not of packing a gun, but of having plenty of men riding behind him who did. Still, if the tales told about him were true, he'd been better than a fair hand with six-gun and rifle himself not too many years past. Noting the fancy pearl-handled revolver on the tooled gunbelt under his fine vest, Glen figured some of that skill was still there.

Rathers opened his mouth to challenge the house again just as Barbara stepped onto the porch. Rathers shut his mouth abruptly.

Barbara's lovely face was pale but determined, and this time she wasn't making any show of concealing the big revolver she held down alongside her dress.

Rathers recovered his composure. ''So, it's the little lady of the house,'' he said in a genial tone that rang as true as fool's gold. ''Have you taken to going armed like some gunslinger, Miss Turner?''

''What do you want?'' Barbara demanded tightly.

Rathers grinned beneath his full gray mustache. ''Just a neighborly visit, miss, checking on your well-being and such.''

Curious, Glen watched the scene, wondering how the rancher was going to play this. The hound stood by and snarled silently.

''We're just fine, thank you,'' Barbara said with unmistakable coldness. ''Now, I really must be about my chores.''

''Not very hospitable to a neighbor, are you?'' Rathers jeered. ''Mighty sorry to keep you from your household duties. We'll just have a word with the man of the house if he's around.'' Scorn edged his words.

''Neither of us have anything to say to you.'' Barbara was standing her ground, Glen thought with admiration.

Rathers settled back some in his saddle, as if reassured now that he was dealing only with a lone woman. ''You could do that little brother of yours a favor,'' he suggested.

''What might that be?''

"Why, just setting him down like a big sister should and giving him some good advice about accepting my offer to buy you folks out. It's a fair deal."

"It may be, but we're not interested in selling."

Rathers ran his glance pointedly over the little homestead. "Lot of work here for a couple of kids," he commented.

Barbara bristled. "Nothing that we can't handle!" she snapped.

"Looks like a passel of work to me," Rathers drawled. " 'Course, I've got plenty of hired hands. If you and little Petey are determined to sticking it out, I suppose I could spare a man now and then to give you some help. How about it, Reno?" He addressed the hard-bitten ramrod. "You willing to lend a hand to the little lady and her brother?"

"Why, sure, Mr. Rathers," Reno responded laconically. "You just say the word, and I'll hustle over in a jiffy."

An ugly chorus of chuckles greeted the comment. Barbara stood very still and straight, as though fearful of letting herself yield even an inch. She bit down hard on her lower lip for a moment. "That won't be necessary," she said then. "Now, I'll have to ask you leave."

"Sure you don't need me to hang around, ma'am?" Reno offered.

"She's sure," Glen said loud enough to carry. "I think you gentlemen have overstayed your welcome."

Startled looks were cast in his direction. Reno turned his horse sharply, hand dropping toward his six-gun. A couple of his cohorts weren't far behind him.

"You're covered!" Glen snapped, and stepped into the open.

He was sighting down the rifle at the broad chest of Reno—the most dangerous one of the lot. His position at the corner of the barn gave him a commanding field of fire and Reno was the first to realize it.

"Hold up, boys!" he ordered sharply. "He's telling the straight of it!"

There was an uneasy shifting of horses. Glen watched for any sudden movement of hand or shoulder.

"You heard Reno," Rathers said, backing his ramrod's command. He didn't look to be upset over Reno's issuing orders. Apparently he knew when to give his top gun free rein.

The gunslicks relaxed a bit. From the edge of his vision Glen saw Barbara's shoulders lift in a visible sigh of relief.

"Who the deuce are you?" Rathers jigged his horse a pace or two in Glen's direction. It moved him clear of the pack and made him the foremost target. Reno sided him at once, but it had still taken some backbone to expose himself to the sights of an unknown rifleman. Above the rancher's gray mustache, dark eyes fixed on Glen with the intensity of a hunting puma's.

"I'm a friend of the lady and her brother," Glen answered.

"It's Glen Douglas, Boss," Reno advised from the side of his mouth. "Used to ride for Judge Parker in these parts."

Rathers frowned thoughtfully. "You got a spread near here, don't you, Douglas?"

"That's right. Me and these folks are neighbors."

"What's your stake in this?"

"I just told you."

Rathers gave an arrogant lift to his chin. "Appears to me you got a lot of gall throwing down on a man making an innocent business offer to a lady."

Glen let it slide. They all knew better than that.

After a space of moments, Rathers shifted uneasily beneath the Winchester's unwavering barrel. He cut a sharp glance at Reno.

"Heard you used to be pretty handy with a six-gun, Douglas," the ramrod said, taking his cue.

"We never crossed paths, or you'd know for sure," Glen told him coolly.

Reno's thin mouth twitched as if he'd heard a joke.

He cocked his head musingly. "That rifle feeling heavy, Douglas? I figure your arms must be getting mighty tired holding it steady that way."

"Good thing your boss doesn't pay you for figuring." Glen's voice was level. Then it sharpened suddenly. "You there! Back into the group!"

The unshaven gunslick who had been edging his

horse away from his bunched cohorts, and into a clear line of fire, scowled before turning his mount back.

Reno's eyes didn't leave Glen at the disturbance, but Rathers cast an angry glare back over his shoulder. "Hold steady, I said!" he barked. Plainly he didn't cotton to the notion of getting caught in the middle of a shooting fest between Glen and his hired guns.

"Look, Douglas," he went on. "You got me wrong. No need for you to be on the prod this way. I offered the lady and her brother a deal, and they turned it down. Fair enough. Reno didn't mean no harm. I think these greenhorn kids are making a mistake by not taking me up on my offer. They don't know a good thing when it's dangled in front of them. But you're cut from a different cloth, I can tell. You've been to see the elephant and gone back again. Am I right?"

"You're doing the talking," Glen said tersely. "But you ain't saying much."

Rathers gave a crisp nod. "All right, I will say something, and you best listen up. I'm willing to make you the same offer I made these fool kids: buy you out for a fair price. That includes livestock, tools, equipment, and fixtures. 'Course, I'll need to look your place over to name an exact amount, but I'm willing to do that today, right now, if you're of a mind to ride over there with us. What do you say to that, Douglas?"

What in tarnation was the man playing at? Glen

wondered. For a moment he was tempted to string along just to try to get an inkling of what Rathers was up to with his offers.

"Not interested," he said aloud as better sense prevailed. "Now, you and your boys ride on off Miss Turner's spread."

The ranch owner's craggy face grew rigid. "You're making a mistake, Douglas," he said with a growl.

"Maybe," Glen said, "maybe not. You'll be making a bigger one if you don't hightail it back to your own range. And Miss Turner and her brother don't need any help from Reno there, or any other of your hands."

"He's got the right of it, Rathers," a new voice intruded with only the slightest trace of uncertainty.

Heads swung toward the sound, and horses shuffled about. Through the pack, Glen glimpsed a sturdy figure in overalls who had appeared at the corner of the house.

"Howdy, Pete," he called. He caught the youth's answering grin. Like his voice, it was a bit strained, but Glen had seen hardened fighting men do worse under similar circumstances.

Pushing eighteen years of age, a few years behind his comely sister, Pete Turner had a tousled head of blond hair and a husky build developed by hard work on their spread. His features were broad and open, just hinting at the strength they might gain with maturity.

Since his pa's death, he'd had to grow up mighty fast. He'd even taken to toting the double-barreled shotgun he now held leveled at the intruders.

Glen let himself ease up a mite. Even with a dead drop, one man bucking a half dozen was heavy odds. But that double-barrel, despite being in the hands of a kid, made all the difference. Glen was glad he'd kept the riders bunched. At that range, Pete's shotgun could do a powerful lot of damage to men and beasts alike.

Reno had bristled up like the snarling hound. He'd let himself be blindsided twice in near as many minutes, and once by a greenhorn kid. That wasn't something a fighting man of his caliber could swallow very easily, Glen knew. But Reno wasn't fool enough to make a play. He shot a look at his boss.

The rancher's piercing eyes had turned murderous. "Don't get too big for your britches, sonny," he snapped at Pete. Then he looked hard at Glen. "And you, cowboy, you ain't always going to have a barn to hide behind."

"I do for now," Glen said coldly.

"You're not welcome here, Rathers." Pete's voice had grown stronger.

Rathers didn't bother to look his way again. "Bring the boys, Reno." He wheeled his big gray smoothly and took off at a canter. His ramrod and the gunslicks fell in behind him. Like a cavalry officer at the head of his troops, Rathers took his motley command away from the house and outbuildings.

Glen lowered his rifle and watched him go. He wiped the frown off his face and went to meet Pete at the steps to the porch.

The young man wore an exhilarated grin. "We made them back water!" he enthused as Glen drew near.

"Good thing they didn't buck us," Glen said tersely.

"Buck us?" Pete exclaimed. "They wouldn't have stood a chance."

"Men like Reno always stand a chance," Glen told him.

Pete sobered. "I was riding up when I saw them," he explained. "Circled wide to come in from behind the house."

"Good move. Glad you showed when you did," Glen praised tersely.

"Those awful men," Barbara interjected. Her face was still pale. "Why would Rathers want to buy us out, anyway?" The hound mounted the porch to stand protectively at her side.

"I guess you met Sis already," Pete spoke up. He beamed proudly at his sibling.

"Reckon I have," Glen confirmed.

"I been wanting to get the two of you introduced proper ever since Sis came home," Pete went on casting a sly grin in his sister's direction. "But she's been too busy taking care of things here. She's quite a housekeeper. Don't recollect as how I've ever seen that cabin look so nice. She'd probably like to have you in to see it. That right, Sis?''

Barbara flushed to the roots of her yellow hair. ''Don't call me that when we have company, Peter,'' she chided, as though eager to change the subject.

Pete grinned and looked back at Glen, a twinkle in his youthful eyes.

''Has Rathers tried this before?'' Glen asked.

Again Pete grew serious. ''Naw. Leastways, he ain't never come riding over here to try to buffalo us before.'' His broad brow furrowed with concern. ''Heard him make you an offer. You don't figure to take him up on it, do you?''

''Not likely.''

Pete relaxed some. ''That's good to hear. We'd hate to lose you as a neighbor.'' He glanced up at the porch where Barbara had busied herself with brushing down a stray cobweb. ''Figure I better do my best to stick close to home when she's here alone, from here on out.''

''I'll give you a hand,'' Glen offered. The prospect of having an excuse to see more of Pete's pretty sister was a nice one, he decided.

''Come on in and let Sis fix us some tea,'' Pete invited.

Glen shook his head in a reluctant refusal. He looked out to the prairie. The buzzards would likely be settling shortly, and he needed to catch the mare again. He still had a grim chore ahead of him, and putting it off wouldn't make it go any easier.

Chapter Three

Glen hammered the last nail into the two-by-six and stepped back with a sigh of satisfaction to admire his handiwork. What with all the other chores and tasks that went with running a one-man spread, it had taken him quite a spell to get the corral finished. Now that it was done, he could start shortly on the horse-breeding operation that had been one of his goals ever since he'd acquired the lease to his homestead.

The afternoon sun was warm on his bare chest. He'd shucked his shirt as the day progressed and the heat increased. Sweat trickled down him, and he used his forearm to wipe it away from his brow beneath the brim of his Stetson. The raw wood of the new boards had a pleasing gleam in the sunlight. It reminded him he still had some painting to do if he wanted to protect the boards from the cantankerous weather of the Indian Lands.

Movement out on the range caught his eye, and he squinted at the mounted figure headed his way. Automatically he shifted hands with the hammer and let his fingertips brush the butt of his holstered Colt. It was rarely beyond his reach of late.

The rider drew closer, and he cocked his head with pleased surprise as he recognized the trim feminine form of Barbara Turner astride the same roan mare he'd borrowed from her the day before. He'd returned the animal after delivering the drygulcher's latest victim to town.

Barbara skirted the corral, riding with a graceful ease. "Afternoon," Glen greeted as she reined up. "Welcome to the Bar D."

She let her eyes rest on him, then quickly ran her gaze over the new corral and the small house and barn that made up the headquarters of his spread. "Why, this is nice," she commented.

Glen noted that she seemed to be having trouble returning her eyes to him. Then the flush in her cheeks made him belatedly remember his partially unclad condition. Hastily he snagged his shirt from the fence where it hung and shrugged into it. She kept her gaze modestly averted as he fastened the buttons and stuffed the shirttails down his britches.

"What brings you over this way?" he asked as he finished.

She looked quickly back at him and smiled with a trace of relief as she saw he was fully clad. "Marshal Manning rode out to our place on his way here to give you a message. I volunteered to deliver it to you since I was already planning on coming this way." She appeared to become a little flustered once again. "I—that is, we—never got the chance to thank you properly for what you did yesterday when Rathers and his men came to our ranch. We wanted to invite you to attend church with us tomorrow morning in town, then have Sunday dinner with us. Do say you will."

He'd been backsliding some in his church attendance of late, Glen reminded himself, and the urging he read in her eyes and her smile was compelling. "I'd be pleased to take you up on that," he told her, and was rewarded with a brightening of her smile. "Light down. I don't have much to offer except some well water at the moment, but you're welcome to a cup."

"That would be wonderful."

She swung down from her saddle with the same lithe ease with which she rode. He saw she wore a divided riding skirt and a frilled white blouse. Her long blond hair had been pulled back and fastened to dangle down her back beneath the flat-brimmed hat she wore.

Taking the reins of her mare, Glen looped them around one of the boards of the corral fence, then led the way to the pump just in front of his porch. He worked the handle, then used the dipper to catch part of the stream of water that poured forth.

"Thank you." As when she'd served him tea, her hand brushed his as she accepted the brimming utensil. "Umm, that's good," she commented in praise after a long sip.

"What's this message the marshal had for me?" Glen asked.

"Oh, I'm forgetful, aren't I?" She took a last sip and returned the dipper.

Glen drained the rest of it. The cold water tasted good to his parched throat, maybe better than usual since her lips had recently touched the same rim. Finished, he hung the wire loop of the dipper back on the nozzle of the pump.

"The marshal wouldn't say much," Barbara explained, "just that the mayor and the Citizens Committee would like to meet with you this evening, if that's convenient."

Glen blinked. "Meet with me about what?"

"I don't know. I thought you might." She appeared to share his perplexity.

Glen frowned. "Haven't the foggiest," he confessed.

She tilted her head, and a spark of mischief danced in her sky blue eyes. "You must be an important man to have the mayor and the Citizens Committee so anxious to meet with you."

Glen felt his lips quirk at her teasing. "Right," he growled dryly.

She gave a pleased little giggle. "You can tell me about it tomorrow. You'll come to our place so we can all ride into town together?"

"I'll be there bright and early."

"Well, then, I'd better be going. I've still got dinner to fix."

"Hold on." Past her, in the distance, Glen could see the blue-hazed ridges of the Arbuckles. With the phantom bushwhacker lurking in those peaks, he didn't cotton to the idea of her riding the prairie alone.

She had paused at his words and was waiting expectantly.

"Let me get cleaned up, and I'll ride with you," he offered. "From your place I can just head on into town. It's getting late enough that I'll have to be leaving here soon anyway in order to get to this mysterious meeting. Besides, with two of us riding together, we'll be safer."

"Okay," she agreed readily. "I'll wait on the porch."

Inside the small cabin, Glen used soap and water and an old washtub before changing into clean clothes. All the time, he was conscious of her presence on the porch just outside. He liked knowing that she was nearby.

She made a pleasant riding companion, almost distracting Glen from keeping his eyes peeled for danger. He noted that shape of her big revolver outlined in her saddlebag. At least she hadn't been riding this range unarmed, he mused, although what good the six-gun would do her against the sharpshooter, he didn't know. For that matter, what good would his own Colt and rifle do? The bushwhacker could strike from far beyond the reach of either.

The ride was over too quickly. He lingered for a spell on her porch, visiting with her, until Pete made his appearance from doing chores. Reluctantly Glen said his good-byes and headed the pinto toward town.

The community of Davis had its origins in the arrival of the Santa Fe Railroad to these parts. Railway officials had made arrangements with Nelson Chigley, a Chickasaw Indian, to divide part of his land into lots at a likely site for a depot. Chigley had donated four lots for use by churches, and S.H. Davis, the town's namesake, had opened his general store on another parcel.

A number of other establishments, including a gunsmith, two livery stables, offices for both Wells Fargo and Western Union Telegraph, a bank, a drugstore with a doctor's office inside, and a saloon now lined the dusty streets. The latter could quickly become muddy tracks during spring and winter rains.

Dusk was falling when Glen rode into town. He passed Garrison's Furniture Store, which also offered a line of caskets. That particular part of the proprietor's business had likely been profitable of late, Glen thought darkly.

He reined in at the marshal's office. As he dismounted, the lawman himself emerged. Along with his age, Oscar Manning was carrying the stress and pressure that went with packing a badge in these parts. He was tall and thin, with a drooping mustache and an air of tiredness that put a slump to his gaunt shoulders.

His lined face lit up with relief as he recognized his visitor. "Glen, glad you could make it!" he said and greeted Glen with a firm handclasp. "I appreciate it; I really do. I guess Miss Turner got word to you all right?"

Glen nodded. "What's this about, Oscar?" He didn't know the man that well, but he respected him as a capable enough law officer for a town like Davis.

Manning bridled. "I better let the Citizens Committee fill you in. They're gathering over at the town hall. That's where I was headed. Come along."

Tamping down his curiosity, Glen accompanied him. The meeting room in the town hall was already crowded when they arrived. Through a haze of cigar smoke Glen picked out a few familiar faces. J.R. Blythe and Henry Richardson, the respective owners of the town's two livery stables, were present, as was W.F. Parker, the druggist, and Dr. Thomas Walker, who officed in his drugstore. S.H. Davis himself had also made an appearance.

Glen cut a glance at Manning, but the lawman was

already hustling forward to mingle with the town fathers. Many eyes turned to Glen, and those men who knew him greeted him affably. He turned down a half dozen offers of a cigar.

As if Glen's arrival had been a signal, Lewis Charters, the mayor, raised his orator's voice to get everyone seated around the conference table or in the chairs that had been drawn up nearby. Glen reversed one of these and straddled it. In all, a dozen or so of the town's premiere citizens had gathered here.

In his honor? Glen wondered. A sneaking suspicion began to rise in him that he was about to be ambushed himself.

Lewis Charters, a practicing attorney when he wasn't busy with his mayor's duties, took his place at the head of the table. He straightened his suit coat and vest, brushed his black mustache with one finger, then slicked graying hair back behind his ears.

"Gentlemen, gentlemen, let's come to order," he suggested peremptorily. Spotting Glen on the outskirts of the gathering, he jerked his head in a beckoning gesture. "Come on in here a little closer, Glen. You're a part of this meeting too."

Glen grinned weakly and obliged him by working his chair a scant couple of inches closer. Charters gave a nod of approval.

"Gentlemen, we've called this meeting to discuss the plague that has settled on our fine community, a scourge that must be stamped out!" he began. The others seemed content to let him do the talking. Glen sensed occasional glances flicked his way. He waited stoically.

"I'm talking of course about the brutal series of murders that has taken the lives of no less than six of our local citizens, Charters continued. "Glen Douglas here himself brought in the latest victim just yesterday: Jacob Parmiter—a good man. And he was not the first."

Charters went on to list the other five victims and extol their virtues, stumbling a little over the identity and good qualities of the first unknown target. "People are getting afraid to come and go from our town," he proclaimed, and drew breath to launch into another chapter.

"Hold on, Lewis," Marshal Manning broke in wearily. "I don't reckon we need to convince Glen how bad matters have gotten. He brought in Parmiter himself, like you said."

"What happened to Parmiter's wife and young 'uns?" Glen broke in to ask.

"They're headed back east," Manning told him. "Mr. Rathers already bought out their place. I figure he'll go ahead and take over their lease with the Chickasaws, like he has with all the rest. What with the pressure to open up the rest of the Lands to settlement, the tribes ain't too interested in leasing out any more than they've already done. Makes it hard for newcomers to these parts."

Glen stored the information away. "What's all this got to do with you inviting me to this meeting?"

Manning sighed. The other men appeared to have accepted his role as the new spokesman. "It's like this, Glen: we need your help, if you're willing to give it."

"What kind of help?"

"Let me put it this way," Manning began. "I was a constable in Chicago before coming out here. I'm pretty good at keeping the peace, handling a few drunks or rowdy cowhands, maybe getting the drop on a would-be robber now and again. But I'm not a manhunter. I can't follow a trail worth shucks. Besides, my jurisdiction ends at the edge of town." Manning paused and drew on a cigar, adding to the haze of smoke in the room.

"These bushwhackings are outside my bailiwick and beyond my abilities," he went on bluntly. "I've made a stab at tracking down the killer and come up empty-handed. I've talked to the tribal police, but they aren't interested in white man's crimes. And I've had a Deputy U.S. Marshal come out. By the time he arrived, it had been a full two weeks since the murder, and he couldn't cut a trail no more than I could. He ended up telling me to get word to the U.S. Marshal's office if there was another killing, and they'd send somebody out. But by the time he gets here, another two weeks will have gone by, and what trail there is will be impossible to follow just like the other time." He dropped the cigar and ground it out underfoot.

Glen recalled Barbara's comment that the marshal's

reluctance to go after the bushwhacker might be due to cowardice. He thought she was wrong. Manning's frustration and despair were evident in his every tone and gesture.

"I'm still waiting to hear what this has to do with me," he said evenly.

"Well, I'll tell you," Manning answered. "You used to ride for Judge Parker. You were one of his best, so I hear tell. You've got the experience and the skills to do what I can't. We—the Citizens Committee—are asking if you'd be willing to track down this drygulcher and put an end to these killings."

Glen had scented this coming down the pike, but he still wasn't sure how to answer. He hesitated, running his eyes over the other men in the room.

"We'd be willing to pay you good wages, maybe even post a reward," Charters offered.

"Give it some thought, Glen," Blake Sedgeman, the dark, saturnine gunsmith, urged.

Images of four men uselessly dead flashed through Glen's mind. He shook his head slowly back and forth. "I'm a rancher. It's been two years since I rode for the judge. That's a long time."

"A manhunter of your caliber never loses the skills," Manning asserted.

"I still don't want any part of bounty hunting. I've put all that behind me."

"We need your help," Charters chimed in.

Glen pulled in a deep breath and let it out. "Whoever's doing this is good—a pro of some sort. No matter what the marshal says, I'm rusty. Even if I went after the bushwhacker, there's no guarantee I could even get close to him. The answer is still no.''

Sighs of disappointment and exchanges of glances among the men at the table greeted his words. Glen shifted uncomfortably on the hard seat of the chair he'd straddled. Could he track down the sharp-shooter if he set himself to the task? he wondered suddenly.

''You got any idea who this killer might be?'' Manning asked shrewdly. ''There's not many who can make the kind of shots he does.''

A chill touched Glen there in the stuffy room. ''I used to know a man who had the eye and the arma-ment to kill like this hombre does. But I haven't heard anything of him since I took off my badge. And,'' he added grudgingly, ''This jasper might've been a cold-blooded killer, but I've never known him to do it out-side the law.''

''Just who is this mankiller?''

''Goes by the name of Quirt,'' Glen said tightly.

Manning's eyes narrowed. ''I've heard that name. If he's the same fellow, then he's bad medicine.''

''He's the same,'' Glen assured him. ''But, like I said, there's nothing to tie him to the drygulchings.''

Manning leaned back with an exhalation of breath. ''I suppose you're right.''

He'd never thought he would hear himself singing

Quirt's virtues, Glen mused wryly. He stood up and swung the chair back around to face forward. "This is work for the U.S. Marshal's office, not me," he said flatly.

As he left the town hall he tried to ignore the troublesome twinge of what he suspected was his conscience.

Chapter Four

Night had crept over Davis when Glen emerged
from the town hall, and his stomach gave a surly growl
to remind him he hadn't eaten since noon. He paused
on the boardwalk, considering. The saloon usually had
a spread of the makings for sandwiches on Saturday
night, and it was both cheaper and faster than the café.
A restless desire to get his belly filled and then leave
the town behind as soon as possible prodded him. He
angled across the road toward the saloon.

The presence of such establishments within the con-
fines of towns like Davis was generally winked at by
the federal authorities. The sale of firewater was pro-
hibited in the Indian Lands.

The usual Saturday night rowdies were in evidence,
Glen noted as he entered. A haze of smoke and dust

hung in the air, laced with the odors of sweat and alcohol. Gaming tables were clustered in the dim recesses of the big room. Customer tables cluttered the floor in front of the bar itself.

Glen's mouth tightened as he noted Jason Rathers and a handful of his crew holding down a table in one corner.

The rancher was slouched in his chair, an open bottle on the table in front of him. He'd apparently staked that whiskey out as his private stock. His hirelings were sharing a couple of bottles of a cheaper brand, with the exception of Reno. The ramrod had his long legs stretched in front of him until he was almost lying in his chair. As Glen watched, Reno reached to snag the higher-priced bottle and pour himself a snort. His boss offered no objection.

Glen did his best to ignore the rancher's brooding stare as he made his way to the buffet. He piled a plate with thick slices of ham, roast beef, and cheese, added a couple of pieces of bread, some hard-boiled eggs, and a generous ladle of beans. A battered fork served as silverware. Left-handed, his right dangling near his Colt, he carried the plate to an empty table, then returned to the buffet for a tin mug of coffee.

As he sat down, he saw Rathers lean forward and speak to his ramrod, who cocked an ear, then let an ugly grin crawl across his weathered features. Rising, Reno swagged across the floor toward Glen. The other patrons made way for him. At his back, Rathers and his cohorts followed his progress with hungry interest.

Glen chomped a bite out of his sandwich, set it back on the plate. He picked up the fork and poised it over the beans as Reno's shadow fell across him. His hand motionless, Glen tilted his head up to eye the ramrod. Reno was spoiling for trouble. Glen reckoned Rathers had sicked the hard case on him.

"You ain't got no barn to hide behind in here, Douglas," Reno said coldly.

"Don't reckon I need one."

"What? You fixing to hide under the table this time?" Reno jeered.

"Nope, just fixing to eat off of it."

"The devil you are!" Reno's hand flicked toward Glen's plate to overturn it.

Like a striking snake, Glen's fork intercepted his hand, the tines sinking in like fangs.

Reno howled and snatched his hand back. Reflexively it reached toward his holstered gun, then stopped rigid as its owner saw the Colt in Glen's hand already canted up at him. The fork lay on the table where Glen had dropped it.

"You're interrupting my dinner," Glen drawled.

Reno was seething like an overheated steam engine. "You pull that trigger and they'll blast you." He jerked his head toward Rather and his companions, a couple of whom had started to their feet in surprise.

"They'll try, but it won't help you any."

Reno ran his tongue over his lips. "Put that hogleg up and let's settle this man-to-man. Fist and boot."

"With all your pards joining in?"

Reno looked over at the table occupied by Rathers and his men. "You boys stay out of this!" he ordered hoarsely. "Tell them, Mr. Rathers."

That's it," Rathers said loud enough to be heard. "Reno's calling this play."

A murmur of excited interest arose from the saloon's other patrons, and was drowned out by the bartender's shouted protest.

"I'll cover the damages!" Rathers overrode him.

Reluctantly the barkeep subsided.

"Well?" Reno demanded, with some of his arrogance returning.

Glen chewed it over. Reno was right; gunplay might be disastrous for them both, and innocent folk could get hurt. But he wasn't about to knuckle under to the segundo's challenge.

"Back off," he ordered, bobbing the barrel of his Colt a bit for emphasis.

Eyes wary, Reno retreated a couple of steps. Then an eager grin creased his face as Glen stood and slid his gun back into the holster. "Fist and boot," he agreed, and circled clear of the table.

He was alert for tricks. Reno lifted his fists and spat at the toe of Glen's boot. Glen recognized in his stance the same sort of hard-earned skill he himself had at this bareknuckle game.

Reno didn't waste any more time. He came in waving his left fist and throwing a long right. Glen hunched his shoulder, got his left arm up and fended off the blow before lashing out in turn with his own right. Reno let his head roll with it, and then, still pressing in, he tried one of the tricks Glen had been half-expecting. He used his foot, swinging it up in a savage kick at Glen's groin.

Glen saw it coming and tried to twist aside. His hip bumped a table, and the toe of Reno's boot drove agonizingly into his thigh. He felt his leg buckle, and hunched both shoulders this time, trying to get his arms up to guard against the hard knuckles he glimpsed flying at his face.

He reeled beneath Reno's battering fists. They bounced off his forearms, caromed off his skull, and set his ears to ringing like the bell on a schoolhouse. Pivoting on his good leg, he got his other planted and saw an opening as Reno's swings became wild. He ripped an uppercut to the stubbled jaw, and threw a shoulder behind it into the ramrod's chest. Reno went back a step to get room, and drove both fists in fast and furious.

Glen was vaguely aware that a kind of arena had been cleared for them in the center of the room. Cheers and catcalls echoed each blow that landed.

And some of Reno's were landing. Glen tried to weather the storm, throwing punches of his own. His bruised leg had robbed him of a bit of his mobility. He stood his ground, figuring Reno would resort to the boot again at some point.

When it came driving up at his groin, Glen was ready. Again he used his good leg to pivot, swinging outside the kick. Off balance, Reno's flying leg sent him lurching forward. From the side, Glen hooked right and left to his head. Reno wobbled. Glen bulled into him, driving him back across the makeshift ring and up against the bar. The flimsy structure shook beneath the impact. Glen glimpsed the barkeep diving for cover.

Reno was growling, trying to get room to strike. Glen used his own foot then, driving it down atop Reno's boot with all the force he could muster. Reno gasped in shock. Glen bore down, trying to grind his foot through the floor.

Then, while Reno was held immobile, almost pegged to the floor, Glen slammed an alternating left and right to his jaw. Bending, he wrapped his arms around Reno's waist and heaved. Pain stabbed his leg as he lifted Reno clear of the floor and dumped him all the way over the bar.

Instantly Glen slapped both palms atop the rough-hewn surface and vaulted it like he was going over a rail fence. Again the ramshackle structure wobbled. Both of Glen's boots came down on Reno's chest. Glen caught his balance, gripped the ramrod's shirt-front, and hauled him erect. Gasping, Reno pawed at him. Glen measured him and swung his right. Reno slammed against the makeshift shelves of bottles at his back. They came down atop him with a crashing of glass and a spray of whiskey as they collapsed. Let Rathers pay for those damages, Glen thought with satisfaction.

He wheeled toward the rancher and his cronies. "Anybody else?" he rasped.

There was a muttering among the hard cases, but Rathers stilled it with a gesture. "Nobody else," he conceded. "Reno called the hand. He played it and lost. Now, I'd like a word with you, Douglas, if you don't mind."

"I don't like the company you're keeping," Glen told him.

"You boys scatter," Rathers ordered. "A couple of you see to Reno."

The hired toughs obeyed without further protest. Curious, Glen moved from behind the bar, crunching glass underfoot. The smell of whiskey seared his nostrils, and his head was starting to ache from Reno's punches. The voices of the other customers began to be raised excitedly in the aftermath of the brawl.

Glen limped across the floor to the rancher's table. Rathers gazed up at him thoughtfully.

"Pretty impressive, Douglas," he said. "Reno's a top hand with guns or fists, but you took him without too much trouble. I reckon you live up to your rep."

Glen shrugged. "Reputations are just words, nothing more."

Rathers gestured at the chair across from him. "Go ahead, take a load off your feet."

Glen circled the table and took another chair that gave him a view of the rest of the room.

Rathers smiled thinly at his caution. He picked up the private bottle and hefted it in one rough hand. ''Have a drink. Best in the house.''

''When I get thirsty, I'll buy my own,'' Glen said coldly. He wondered what trail Rathers was headed down with this sociable talk.

The rancher took no offense at his refusal. ''Fair enough.''

''What's on your mind, Rathers?'' Glen prodded. ''I still haven't eaten my dinner.''

Rathers poured himself a drink, then downed it. ''I hear the Citizens Committee was looking to hire you to go after the bushwhacker.''

''You hear all sorts of things,'' Glen said noncommittally.

''But this is true,'' Rathers spoke with assurance, then leaned forward intently. ''Did you take them up on their offer?''

''What's it to you?''

Rathers relaxed a little and spread his hands peaceably. ''Just a civic-minded citizen of these parts. The bushwhackings are bad for the town and the region. Gives it a bad name; hurts everybody.''

''You seem to be profiting by them.''

The rancher's eyes went narrow. ''What's that supposed to mean?''

''Just a comment. You seem to be buying up the holdings of every victim.''

"I'm a good businessman. I know enough to take advantage of opportunities when they come my way. Most of the victims' families have been happy to sell to me."

Glen held his tongue, studying the older man closely.

Rathers didn't look to be disturbed by this line of talk. "I'm figuring you didn't take that job the Citizens Committee offered," he said shrewdly. "Am I right?"

"Figure what you want."

Rathers smiled in triumph. "Doesn't matter to me, one way or another, except you might be just a little more willing to listen to my proposition if you're not already tied up with a wild goose chase for that fool Committee."

"What proposition?" Glen asked bluntly.

"Let me put you on my payroll. Among other things you could be my bodyguard in case the bushwhacker starts gunning for me. I'll pay you top gunman's wages. You can even keep working your spread, just so long as you're available to lend a hand when I need you for a job."

"Like maybe rousting Pete Turner and his sister?"

Rathers shrugged carelessly. "I'll make my own deal with those blamed kids. You won't be involved if you're squeamish. I just want you on tap in case of trouble, or to ride the trail with me if I'm passing close to the Arbuckles. I have to be careful. I've got lots of enemies."

"So I'd figure," Glen commented dryly.

Rathers ignored the gibe. "Well, what about it?" he demanded.

Glen leaned back in his chair so he could get on his feet if need be without tangling himself up with the table. The hard cases had left the saloon, taking Reno with them.

"I'm waiting," Rathers said with an edge of irritation.

"This is the second time you've tried to buy me," Glen said deliberately. "My place isn't for sale, and neither am I." He shook his head slowly. "I wouldn't work for you on a bet. I've seen the way you operate. You turned your hounds loose on a couple of young folks, and you sicked the sorry pack leader on me. If I worked for you, I wouldn't ever be able to sleep at night, and I couldn't look at myself in the mirror in the mornings. You made me a couple of offers. Well, I'll make you just one. Lay off of Pete Turner and his sister, or I'll take your crew apart like I just did your foreman."

Rathers's face went taut, the skin drawing back over the bones until his teeth were bared. "If that's the way of it, then listen up," he gritted. "Nobody bucks me, not you and not old man Turner's filthy whelps. I've staked out my trail and I'm riding down it. Don't get in my way!"

"I'm already in your way, and right in the middle of your trail." Glen stood up and moved away from the table. He could feel the rabid glaring eyes of the rancher fixed on him.

His plate still sat untouched on the table he'd deserted. Left-handed, he picked it up and strode out of the saloon. Rathers could pay for his dinner, too.

Chapter Five

"Let us close with a passage from the Ninety-first Psalm." The pastor's compelling voice rolled over the crowded sanctuary. "It is a promise we can all take comfort in during these troubled times: 'Thou shalt not be afraid for the terror by night; nor for the arrow that flieth by day.' Now, let us pray."

Dutifully, Glen bowed his head. He barely heard the preacher's supplications to the Lord. These days it wasn't arrows the local folks needed to fear; it was .50-caliber slugs fired by a marksman with the devil's own skill. Glen offered up his own prayer that the Lord's promise would hold true against the bush-whacker's rifle as well.

They sang a final hymn after the prayer. Beside Glen, Barbara's voice rose pure and sweet. She was appealing, with her hair done up, and wearing a demure ruffled dress over a rustling petticoat. Watching her surreptitiously, as he had throughout the service, Glen noted that her pretty features had taken on a kind of spiritual beauty in the peaceful radiance that seemed to shine from her.

The beauty still hadn't faded as they emerged from the church with others of the departing congregation. Not too long before, the church meetings had been held in the schoolhouse nearby. But a fine new building had recently been finished, complete with gleaming white steeple.

Barbara slipped her arm through Glen's, which he crooked obligingly. Her soft touch made his blood rush, and the smile she gave him made him catch his breath.

"I'm so happy you came with us!" she enthused.

Glen was pretty happy himself. He had enjoyed her company as well as the church service. As always, the congregation was warm and friendly. Barbara, a relative newcomer to the community, didn't look to be having any trouble endearing herself to the local folk. And even those members of the Citizens Committee who were present had been open and amicable.

Glen grinned when he spotted young Pete Turner engaged in earnest conversation with a pretty teenage girl. They stood close together beneath the spreading limbs of a stately oak tree that shaded part of the church grounds.

Motion in the street drew Glen's eye. Traveling at a good clip, a one-horse farm wagon was headed into town from out on the prairie. Something in the urgency of the driver's efforts to get more speed out of the old plow horse in the traces made the hackles rise along the back of Glen's neck.

Barbara must've felt the sudden tension in his muscles, for abruptly she turned a sobering face to him. "What's wrong?"

"I don't know," Glen said tightly. But he was afraid he had all too good of an idea.

He had told Barbara and Pete about the ruckus at the saloon, downplaying the brawl with Reno. And he had told them of the request made by the Citizens Committee.

"The nerve of them!" Barbara had exclaimed. "Why should you risk your life to bring in this killer?"

"It's what I used to do for a living," Glen pointed out. He wondered why he was defending the Committee anyway.

"Well, you don't do it anymore!" Barbara responded archly. "I'm glad you told them no."

He was touched by her evident concern for him, but doubts about his refusal were beginning to nag him.

Now, seeing the wagon pull up in front of the marshal's office, he felt a grim tightness clutch his gut. Wordlessly he watched as the farmer scrambled out of the buckboard and bolted through the doorway into the building. Vaguely he realized Barbara was gripping his arm very tightly.

In a few moments the tired figure of Oscar Manning appeared, followed by the driver. With an air of apprehension the lawman rounded the wagon and lifted the edge of a tarp covering something in the wagon's bed. He studied the object only briefly before he gave a weary shake of his head and let the tarp fall.

"Stay here," Glen said quietly.

"No," she answered in a hushed voice. "I'm going with you."

She clung to his arm as he threaded his way clear of the churchgoers and slanted across the street toward the wagon. Manning glanced around and saw them coming. A scowl darkened his aging features. Glen recognized the hovering driver as Floyd Tull, a local dirt scrabble farmer. Tull started to speak up excitedly, but Manning waved him to silence.

"Who is it?" Glen asked tonelessly as they draw near.

"Jeffrey Webster," Manning told him.

"The bushwhacker again?"

"See for yourself." Manning moved aside.

Glen eased his arm free from Barbara's fingers and stepped to the wagon. He pulled the tarp back and gazed down without speaking for a long moment. "It's Jeffrey Webster, all right," he confirmed. Behind him he heard Barbara moan.

Webster had been making a go of running cattle on

a nice piece of pastureland in the shadow of the Arbuckles. He'd probably been dead before he hit the
ground. A direct hit from a Sharps could drop a buffalo; a man didn't stand a chance.

Glen looked at Tull. "Where did you find him?"

The young farmer was chomping at the bit to talk.
His words came out in a rush. "Smack-dab in front
of his own soddy. Must've got him when he come out
first thing this morning. I was stopping by just to say
howdy when I found him. Shot had to come from
eight, nine hundred yards away up in the mountains.
Wasn't no sign of anyone having come on his place—
just him laying there. Good thing he didn't have no
wife or kids."

Glen let go of the tarp. He felt Manning's gaze on
him and met it levelly. After a pair of seconds the
lawman eased his gaze over toward the church. Tull's
excited tones had begun to attract the attention of some
of the people still lingering in front of the building.
By twos and threes they were drifting in their direction.

"Marshal," Glen said.

Manning turned his head back. "Yeah?"

"You can tell Charters and the rest of them that I'll
take them up on their offer. But I won't do it for
money."

A small stifled sound of protest came from Barbara.
Manning gave a sigh of relief and nodded. "I'll tell
them."

Barbara's hands closed on his arm as he allowed himself to be drawn away from the townspeople converging on the wagon and its gruesome cargo.

"Why, Glen?" Barbara swung herself around to face him. Her voice was quiet and insistent. "Why did you agree to do it?"

"Because somebody has to, and maybe I'm the best qualified."

"But you could be killed!"

"I could get killed if I stay here. Eventually the bushwhacker will pick me for a target. Or you. Or Pete."

She shuddered and pressed her teeth against her lower lip. Her hands clenched into fists. "Why is this happening?" she cried softly.

"I don't know for sure," Glen said darkly, "But I know who's benefiting from it."

Her eyes opened wide. "What do you mean?"

"I mean Jason Rathers is taking over the holdings of each victim of the drygulcher. It's my guess that, in addition to buying up whatever he can of the victims' possessions—equipment and such—that he's going to the Chickasaws and negotiating to take over the leases as well."

"But why?"

"I'm still figuring about that," Glen admitted. "Seems an awful lot of trouble to go to just to increase holdings that aren't guaranteed to last beyond the terms of the leases."

Once more he chewed over a possible motive. Most folks, himself included, planned to continue to lease their land from the tribe in hopes of eventually being able to purchase it. The free homesteads from the Land Run in Oklahoma Territory to the east were long gone, snatched up by the sooners and those who'd made the run. Good land there now went for top dollar. Taking a gamble on the low rent of Indian land seemed a good risk for a man short on *dinero*. But it didn't stack up as a sure enough bet to justify killing your neighbors off right and left. Glen shook his head in frustration.

"Do you think Jason Rathers is the bushwhacker?" Barbara's question pulled him out of his reverie.

"No," he answered her, "but I think he could've hired somebody who is staying up in the mountains and picking off local farmers and ranchers when he has the chance."

"How horrible! Can't you go to the marshal?"

"You tried it," Glen reminded her, "and it didn't get you anywhere. Manning's a part of the Citizens Committee, and they want me to corral this yahoo. The marshal's in over his head; even he admits that. Besides, I don't have any proof that Rathers is behind it—just a nasty hunch."

"But why do you have to go after the killer yourself?" Won't the marshal put together a posse to hunt him down?"

"A posse of townfolk and ranchers would never catch him in the mountains. One man has a better chance. Whoever he is, he'd run rings around a posse, maybe even pick them off one by one at his leisure. Believe me, he could do it.'' Glen realized he was speaking as if he knew for a certainty that the sharp-shooter was Quirt.

''Won't he do the same thing to you?'' Barbara persisted bluntly.

''I'm a lot smaller target than a whole posse. And I know how to move around in those mountains without being seen. Remember I used to earn my keep hunting down men like this. And, mostly, I worked alone.''

''But that was a long time ago!''

''Not so long,'' Glen denied quietly.

But a calculating voice in the back of his mind told him what she said was true. He had begged off to the Citizens Committee with the excuse that he was rusty. How rusty was he? Quirt—if it was Quirt—would be as good as he'd ever been at stalking human prey. Maybe better.

Resolutely, Glen shrugged off his doubts. He had no choice. What he had told Barbara was true too. If he didn't get the bushwhacker, then, he was sure, the bushwhacker would eventually get him. Or Barbara.

''Where are you going?'' she exclaimed as he wheeled away. ''You were supposed to have dinner with us.''

''I can't; not now. It's important that I get out to Webster's spread as soon as possible and see if I can pick up a trail. I'll have to go by my place first and get outfitted.''

He paused at the stricken look on her face. ''I'm sorry,'' he said honestly. ''This won't happen next time.''

She nodded mutely and swallowed hard. When she spoke, her voice was tremulous. ''Be careful.''

''I will.'' Glen had the sudden impulse to take her in his arms and reassure her. For a heady moment he fancied she wanted the same thing. But the main street of Davis on a Sunday morning were hardly the time and place for such carryings-on, even if they were proper between two people who had know each other only a handful of days.

And, the same calculating voice told him remorselessly, any reassurances he gave her would be less than honest. He couldn't promise that there ever would be a next time to attend church with her, or have lunch with her, or hold her in his arms.

''Sis, Glen, what's wrong with you two?'' Pete Turner had spotted them and left the crowd of gawkers gathered around Tull's wagon. His boyish features showed puzzled concern as he looked back and forth between the pair.

''I'm going after the drygulcher,'' Glen told him flatly. ''I'll likely be gone a few days. While I am, keep a watch on your sister and my homeplace.''

''I'll go with you!'' Pete exclaimed as if he hadn't heard anything beyond Glen's stated intent.

"No, Peter!" Barbara objected sharply.

But two of us will have a better chance than one!" Pete retorted. "Right, Glen?"

"No," Glen told him flatly. "I have to do this alone. The best way you can help is to stay here and do what I just told you."

Pete scowled and balled his fists in evident frustration. At last his shoulders sagged with resignation. "All right." His acceptance was grudging.

Glen gave a crisp nod and swung away to head toward where the pinto waited patiently tethered to the Turners' wagon in front of the church. His mind was going at a gallop as he tallied up the preparations that were needed for his trek.

Back at his cabin he hurriedly loaded supplies in a gunny sack, then more carefully looked over his gear and ammo. Pete would see to the necessary chores around his place; painting the corral would have to wait. . . .

He lifted his field glasses and thumbed them into focus. Dark memories stirred in him as he recalled other times he'd used them to focus on human prey. He'd been wrong when he'd turned in his badge. He hadn't been able to put the manhunting trade behind him after all.

The day was further along than he would've liked when he rode out. Daylight was precious if he was to get a hot scent. He headed cross-country toward Webster's spread. The upthrusting peaks of the Arbuckles loomed closer as he rode.

A couple of times he stopped long enough to pull out the field glasses and scan the face of the mountain range. Once he saw a bounding speck of white that he knew to be a mountain goat plunging precipitously from crag to crag. He spotted no trace of humanity, but he was aware that the harsh fastness of the peaks could easily hide an army of bushwhackers.

In a grove of cottonwoods a hundred yards from Webster's homestead, he took a spell to scan the mountain faces again. He was within long rifle range of the peaks now, as Webster's death proved. There was an off chance that the killer was still lurking nearby.

Up this close the harsh crags and planes and ridges of the mountains became more evident. Though only a small range, the Arbuckles made up in sheer ruggedness what they gave way in size. Pine forest and scrub brush clothed many of the peaks, giving them a dull emerald beauty in the afternoon sunlight. Other crags stood naked and barren, thrusting up arrogantly toward the sky.

Rockslides were a constant danger, and heavy rains could turn the steep-sided ravines and gullies into raging torrents in only minutes. Travel on horseback for extended distances was impossible. No roads penetrated into the interior of the range, and only the most meager of trails snaked through the tangled forests of trees and rocks.

Glen begrudged the time spent studying the peaks,

but he didn't want to walk into the sharpshooter's sights this early in the hunt. At last, as satisfied as he was likely to get under the circumstances, he remounted and rode out of the cottonwoods. Swinging wide, he approached the soddy from the rear.

He dismounted and slipped around the sod structure, feeling a curious prickle as he came into what he knew had been the bushwhacker's target zone. But no big slugs came his way; no distant shots rang out. Grimly he put himself to examining the area.

Tull's conclusions had been pretty much on the money, he judged shortly. Webster must've been shot when he stepped out of the soddy. The drying bloodstains told the tale.

Once more Glen unshipped his field glasses. Standing in front of the sagging building he studied the mountain faces with painstaking care, trying to pinpoint the most likely spot from which the fatal bullet had flown. Any number of outcroppings and ledges offered good possibilities, but the bushwhacker would've wanted substantial cover, an easy escape route, and a clear field of fire. That narrowed the choices considerably.

At last Glen lowered the glasses and squinted at the spot he'd settled on. A rocky promontory jutted from a wooded mountainside some eight hundred yards distant. For a rifleman with the killer's skill and armament it made a perfect sniper's perch for targeting the Webster homestead.

Glen realized his teeth were grinding together. He let his jaws relax and mounted the pinto. In the saddle, he took one last look around the place. There were chores to be done, and livestock to be tended to, but he knew neighbors would take care of those tasks. Either that, he added darkly, or Jason Rathers would see that it was done.

Staying to cover as much as possible, Glen rode toward the mountains.

Chapter Six

Baffled, Glen squatted on his haunches and studied the faint traces in the dust atop the rocky promontory overlooking the Webster homestead. A man might've knelt there and sighted down a long barrel at a tiny figure below. Or the marks could've been left by a passing mountain goat, or even have been caused by the vagaries of the wind twisting and curling around the peaks.

Scowling, Glen stared down at the little soddy. It was in shadow now, but he could imagine the carefully aimed Sharps centering on the front door in expectation of its target coming into view. Allowance would've been made for wind—not much in the early morning—and droppage of the bullet in flight. Withal, it would've been a fairly easy shot.

Glen rocked back on his heels. He was certain the killer had made the shot from this very site. But he had done it and departed leaving nary a trace of his presence. Glen looked over his shoulder at the woods close behind him. His work done, the drygulcher could've faded back into the trees and gone up or down or in either direction along the steep grade.

Tracking him wouldn't be easy, and the sun was already low, its rays no longer penetrating to the forest floor on this side of the mountain. If a trail had been left, he wouldn't have much luck picking it up today, Glen concluded. He needed to find a spot to hole up for the night, and he needed to be careful in doing it. He could easily become the prey in this stalking game.

He returned to the pinto, which he had been forced to leave farther down the grade. The black and white coloring of the beast made him stand out as a target, but he was surefooted as a puma, and no stranger to bearing riders about these mountains. Having a horse of his breed under a man could mean the difference between life and death for a manhunter in the Arbuckles, Glen knew from harsh experience.

Leading the horse, he moved higher up the slope, finally hobbling him in a small grassy clearing. His saddle and blanket he left nearby concealed under a tarp. Toting his bedroll, gear, and supplies, he moved cautiously upslope, leaving the pinto behind. As the four outlaws had learned those years before, the nearness of a horse could be a dead giveaway to the rider's presence.

In the shelter of a tangled thicket of underbrush, with a sheer cliff face to protect his back, Glen made a cold camp. As darkness settled, he chewed on jerky and sipped from his canteen. The blackness seemed to creep into the thicket. Gradually, branches and foliage that had been plainly visible in the dusk faded from view. He found himself staring futilely into the darkness, trying to discern its secrets.

He thought of the old tales and legends of these mountains: of the ancient Spanish mines abandoned by the conquistadors; of the thirteen muleloads of Spanish gold said to be hidden in one of the caves honeycombing the peaks; of gnarled trees carved with emblems of tortoises and frogs to mark mineral outcroppings; of the cannon stuffed with gold and dumped in the creek when Indians attacked, its location said to be marked by a silver plate. Ghosts haunted the Arbuckles. For a fact, Glen knew that Jesse James had hidden out here in the old days, and even was rumored to have buried loot from one of his robberies in these parts. How many men had died here over the years, victims of the elements or other men, their stories forever lost? Glen wondered.

Far off in the night a puma screamed, harsh and echoing. As if startled by the sound, something moved in the thicket nearby, something large. Glen heard the rustling of branches as it retreated. He caught a whiff of a harsh scent that might've come from a bear; he couldn't be sure.

He shook his head to dispel the lingering specters out of the mountains' past. There were enough real dangers without his mind conjuring up imagined ones.

He spread his bedroll and stretched out. He could feel the comforting metal of the Winchester under his palm as he dozed off.

Suddenly he came back into awareness. He was not sure what had roused him. Maybe it had been a sound; maybe some deep feral instinct. He sat up, the rifle coming smoothly to hand. He was levering it even as his eyes took in the gaunt figure rising out of the dim brush like one of the old ghosts given flesh and substance.

His Winchester came in line, his finger firm on the trigger, in the same instant that he saw the huge rifle in the figure's hands, leveled likewise at him.

Stalemate. Mexican standoff. If either man fired, both of them would die.

The moon had risen to cast a wan illumination into the thicket. It was bright enough for Glen to recognize the grimly familiar buckskinned form holding the Sharps rifle dead on him. His gut went taut with the certain knowledge that he had been right all along.

''Now let's just both sit easy, Deputy,'' the grating voice drawled. Quirt too had seen and understood the significance of their standoff.

''Put that cannon down,'' Glen advised tersely.

''No sir, Deputy, I don't think so.'' Some distortion

of the moonlight caught the bounty hunter's eyes and made them seem to glow like those of a predatory beast.

Glen couldn't move without risking the withering discharge of the giant buffalo gun. At this range there was no way he would survive it. But Quirt likewise was trapped by the repeating Winchester centered on him.

Quirt's chuckle rang sepulchrally. "We got us a right pretty fix, don't we, Deputy?"

How had the bounty man managed to find him? Glen bleakly asked himself.

"Saw you from a distance riding into the mountains." Quirt might've read his mind. "Thought it was you, and figured maybe we better have a confab. That's going to be hard with us pointing guns at one another, each of us waiting for the other to shoot."

Glen didn't answer. Sweat was cold on him. He had to fight the automatic impulse to curl his finger a little bit tighter on the trigger.

"What do you say we handle it like this?" Quirt went on companionably. "Let's both just put our guns down so we can talk like civilized men and walk away alive when we're done."

Glen chewed it over. He had his enemy under his sights. It went against the grain to just lay his gun aside. But he couldn't see any other way of coming out of this confrontation alive. Even going along with Quirt's plan didn't make it a sure thing.

"You call," he said tightly.

"Okay, okay," Quirt said softly with some satisfaction. "On the count of three, both of us at the same time. Ready now?"

Could he trust Quirt to carry out his own plan? He had no choice. He wished the light were better so he could read Quirt's gaunt face more clearly.

"One . . . two . . . three."

Slowly Glen eased his gun aside as Quirt did the same. He had to force his fingers to uncurl from the Winchester. Quirt still wore a six-gun, as did he, but the bounty man was known only for his prowess with a long gun, not as a fast-draw artist. Maybe Glen still had an edge.

"I got to say, you're still mighty good, Deputy." Quirt hunkered down, careful to keep his hands well clear of the discarded Sharps. He used his left to dig through the tangled mane of his hair and scratch hard at his scalp like a dog with the mange. "What are you doing up in these misbegotten hills, anyway?"

"Looking for you."

For a moment Quirt's hunched figure was very still. "Is that a fact now? And why would you be doing that?"

"You're the bushwhacker, aren't you, Quirt?" Glen accused softly. "You're the one that's been picking off the farmers and ranchers from up on the peaks."

"Am I?" Quirt's chuckle was hollow.

"Yeah, you are. The question is, why? You walked

the boundary line, but you never crossed over into being the same kind of man you hunted. But you have now.''

''What's it to you if I have? I heard you turned in that tin badge you used to set so much store by.''

''You've killed some people I knew, and counted as friends and neighbors. Besides, any decent man given the chance has an obligation to stop a cold-blooded killer.''

Had Quirt lived alone here in the Arbuckles for the last two years? Glen queried suddenly to himself. Had the solitude and the loneliness simply brought to the fore that bloodthirsty killing madness that had always lurked so near the surface? Quirt shifted a bit, bringing his face out of shadow. The play of moonlight gave his haggard, furry features the look of a stubbled skull.

''So you reckon you can stop these killings, do you, Deputy?''

''I reckon,'' Glen said with conviction. ''But you still haven't answered my question. Are you the killer?''

''Why, I'd be a fool to admit to being the killer to a man like you. Shoot, Deputy, you're still a lawman down in your gut where it counts. That ain't changed.''

''What about you?'' Glen countered. ''Have you changed?''

Quirt shook his head slowly back and forth. ''Not so much, I've always been willing to drop the hammer on any man that's got a bounty on his head.''

"These aren't outlaws. They're farmers and ranchers, decent folk."

"Reckon it's all in the eye of the fellow posting the bounty, ain't it?"

An icy gun barrel seemed to touch the back of Glen's neck. "So you've crossed over," he accused tautly. "You're nothing but a hired killer."

"That's all I've ever been, Deputy. Didn't you know? You and me, and men like us, cleared out most of the outlaws. A man's got to make a living, and the government ain't posting many bounties these days."

"Who is?" Glen demanded silently. "Who's paying you, Quirt?"

The bony shoulders lifted in a shrug. "That don't matter, so long as I do get paid. You never understood."

"Maybe not. But I can't let you keep on."

Quirt's head tilted up and down in a slow nod. "That's what I figured when I saw you come riding up here. But I thought I better make sure. No point in us getting crossways of each other unless we have to."

"We have to," Glen said evenly.

"That's a shame; it purely is. I always kind of respected you. I never knowed you to start out after a man and not bring him down. Just like me."

"Not like you."

" 'Course, there's got to be a first time for everything." Quirt's voice hardened suddenly, the sham affability slipping away. "And I ain't never forgot the

way you hornswoggled me out of them bounties that
was rightfully mine. Wiring the judge not to pay them
was a nasty trick. I figure I owe you for that.''

''Give it up, Quirt.'' Glen knew the words were
useless.

''Don't come after me,'' Quirt warned. ''We hit a
stalemate this time; you got lucky. It won't happen
again. Fair warning. It's the only one you'll get.''

''You're not interested in the money anymore, are
you, Quirt?'' Glen said with bleak insight. ''It's the
stalk and the kill. The money's just an excuse.''

Quirt didn't answer. His hunched form had a feral,
bestial aspect to it. Gingerly, so it was clear he wasn't
fixing to fight, he reached out to pick up the Sharps.
Just as slowly Glen took up the Winchester. He knew
both guns were still primed to fire. The standoff held.
The wrong move would still get both men killed. Glen
eased to his feet. Quirt straightened to his full bony
height.

''So long, Deputy.''

One moment Quirt was there, and the next he had
vanished like a wisp of powdersmoke. Glen dropped
the Winchester and hurled himself to the left, his right
hand snaking out his Colt even as he moved. A thundering spike of flame erupted from the brush where
Quirt had disappeared. In midair Glen felt the rush of
the big slug go by him. The fingers and thumb of his
gun hand convulsed, and the Colt bucked in his grip
before he hit the ground. From right to left he raked
the underbrush with .45 slugs.

Instinctively he had known Quirt would cut loose with the bushwhacker's gun as soon as he was out of Glen's view. And Quirt would've expected him to open fire with the Winchester. He might not have expected him to use the six-gun in this fashion.

The hammer clicked on an empty shell casing. Glen snatched the Winchester and rolled up on one knee. He stabbed three more shots into the undergrowth for good measure, then dropped flat.

His ears were ringing, and powdersmoke teared his eyes and burned his throat. On his belly he wriggled forward. Most times in this type of deadly game, the man who waited and played it patient had an advantage. But Quirt had been too near, too close to being in Glen's hands, for him to let the bounty hunter slip away if he could help it.

He writhed into the brush, using the rifle to fend branches from his face. He was conscious he had not taken time to reload the Colt, although he'd had the presence of mind to slide it back into the holster.

Thirty feet into the growth he stopped. A sour disappointment rose in him. If he had dropped Quirt with his barrage of lead, he felt sure he would've found him by now. Somehow, uncannily, the drygulcher had evaded his return fire and vanished like a wraith.

Where was he? Still skulking nearby? Glen tended to doubt it, but he didn't plan on taking any chances. Now, at night, in terrain with which Quirt was more familiar, was no time to outmaneuver him. Stealthily

Glen crept back toward his campsite. He stayed in the brush for a time, fearing Quirt might have doubled back, before he ventured out to retrieve his gear and bedroll.

Moving on foot in the darkness was a slow and hazardous proposition. Unseen rocks could turn underfoot, or a misstep could result in a plunge into a crevasse or fissure. Warily, his senses alert, he worked his way at an angle up the steep grade until he found a small overhang created by a jutting ledge. In its shelter he spread his bedding and settled in for what was left of the night.

His sleep was more a series of catnaps than actual slumber. First light found him slipping through the timber to the small clearing where he'd left the pinto. The pony grazed unmolested, and Glen breathed a sigh of relief. At least Quirt hadn't found his mount.

Leading the pinto, he returned to his original campsite of the night before. He hobbled the horse and penetrated the undergrowth from which Quirt had emerged. A few small broken limbs and a scuff mark in the thin soil were the only signs he could find of the bounty hunter's presence. But the direction of the break and the placement of the scuff mark were enough to convince him that Quirt had quit the area rather than trade gunfire in such tight quarters.

The brush petered out on a sheer rocky slope after about fifty or sixty yards. Quirt's Apache moccasins hadn't left even so much as a scuff mark, but Glen was certain he had passed this way in his retreat.

Frowning, Glen studied the lay of the land. Moving fast at night, Quirt would've stayed to the easier goings. Farther down the barren slope, a wooded draw dropped into a rocky canyon. Quirt, familiar with the terrain, would likely have chosen that route to depart the area. Glen's eyes ranged over the far wall of the canyon. It was rugged gray stone, scarred and distorted by upthrusting ridges, narrow ledges, and perilous outcroppings. An active man of Quirt's skills could've scaled it even at night.

Glen was confident he had found Quirt's escape route. He used the field glasses to study it in more detail. Then he swung the lenses in a wider arc. He had no intention of blindly following Quirt's suspected path. But a man on a good horse could circle the rim of the canyon to reach the far side.

Swinging the glasses in the other direction, Glen was a bit surprised to see the open ground of the plains just beyond the neighboring peak. He was not as deep into the range as he had imagined. He had forgotten how the Arbuckles could become a world unto themselves once a person set foot in them. In this terrain where the land had been stood on edge, the surrounding prairie seemed remote and somehow beyond reach.

He headed back for the pinto, pausing only to slake his thirst at a cool stream. He gnawed gamely on a piece of jerky to quiet his belly. In the saddle, he skirted the thicket to return to his vantage point so as not to lose his bearings. After a time, the wooded slopes and looming cliff faces had a tendency to take on a confusing sameness. More than one prospector, emerging from the Arbuckles with tales of a rich strike, had been doomed to a lifetime of fruitless searching by his inability to retrace his steps to his find.

Shielded by the brush, Glen made a mental map of the route he intended to follow. Then he cast another glance to the far rim of the canyon.

His eye caught the flicker of movement. He tensed, yearning for his field glasses, but unwilling to take his eyes off the spot where he'd detected motion long enough to bring the lenses into play. He was telling himself it could've been a coyote or puma when a human figure—tiny in the distance—passed briefly into view.

Glen came out of the saddle and eased forward, Winchester half raised in his grip. With his heart thumping in his chest, he calculated range and distance. It would be a tricky shot for the Winchester, but he just might make it, given another chance.

A long couple of minutes dragged past. Then once more the figure appeared. There was no mistaking the faded dun color of Quirt's buckskins. Eagerness to finish this ugly business pumped hard in Glen. He lifted the Winchester, sighted carefully on that distant form, and fired. The barrel kicked up a few inches from recoil. He lowered it, fired again, and realized in one awful beat of time that he'd played into Quirt's hands like a greenhorn.

He started to dodge just as he saw the tiny puff of smoke. Then something caught him in the ribcage with a jolt that spun him aside and down. Fear and anger clawed at him. He had been a fool to try for Quirt from this distance. Both of his shots had almost certainly missed. The gap across the canyon was at the extreme range for his Winchester. But the range wasn't extreme for the Sharps in Quirt's hands, particularly if it was fitted with scope and mounted sights.

Guessing at Glen's location, hoping to lure him into taking a shot that in all likelihood would miss, Quirt had deliberately drawn Glen's fire so the powder-smoke would give him a target for the Sharps.

And he'd hit his target. Glen didn't know how bad he was hurt; he was a little surprised to find himself still alive and kicking. Desperately he scrabbled for cover in the underbrush, somehow managing to hold onto his rifle the while. A massive wasp seemed to tear through the leafy branches over his head. The sound of the distant report was lost in the harshness of his own panting breath.

Mentally, Glen berated himself. He'd never have made such a fool mistake back when he'd worn a badge. He was rustier than he'd ever imagined.

But he knew he could waste little time on such re-criminations if he wanted to survive. The Good Lord had indeed protected him from the big .50-caliber shell. But he himself was going to have to do some scrambling if he wanted to get out of this alive.

Weak and staggering, he reached the pinto. The thicket provided a screen of cover. The horse shied briefly, then stilled as Glen got a handful of its mane. For a moment he sagged, clinging to the saddle to hold himself upright. The scent of horseflesh, strong and rank, filled his nostrils. Fumbling, he shoved the Winchester into its scabbard.

Quirt would be headed this way to make sure of his kill, but Glen spared precious moments to cut a long strip from the burlap sack and bind it tightly about his chest. For now, his makeshift doctoring would have to serve.

Half of his body seemed to be growing numb. He had to flop across the saddle from the wrong side, and twist and heave himself about until he got astride the pinto.

With clumsy fingers, and with sweat blurring his vision, he lopped the reins about both wrists and bound them to the saddle horn, hunching over to use his teeth to pull the knot tight. In his weakening condition, he was afraid he'd never get back in the saddle if he should fall off the horse. Better to risk being dragged than to wait helplessly for Quirt to find him if he did fall.

He headed the pinto through the brush, emerging at last on the summit of a steep slope of naked stone that dropped down to the grassland he had glimpsed earlier. Patches of loose rock and gravel marred the surface of the grade. A fringe of trees along the near edge would offer some protection from Quirt's probing eyes.

He knew he had to get out of the mountains and try to reach a sawbones. The precipitous slope offered the quickest route. He could only pray that Quirt wasn't anyplace where he would have a clear shot.

He put heels to the pinto. The horse balked, then, with a fretful snort, lurched down the slope. The world dropped away before Glen's eyes. He leaned far back in the saddle so as not to overbalance his mount.

The pinto's descent, of needs, was a series of downward plunging leaps, speed alone keeping the animal from going end over end. Glen felt the powerful surge of his mount's body beneath him. He glimpsed sparks flying as the pony's shod hooves struck naked stone.

Gravel sprayed then from beneath those hooves as they hit a stretch of loose stone. His purchase gone, the pinto folded his hind legs desperately beneath him. Squatting like a dog, forelegs out stiff in front, he slid through the gravel. Glen had impressions of the animal's wildly rolling eyes, of the sky and ground seeming to heave around him. He reeled in the saddle, trying to cling with his legs. He realized remotely that, without the binding reins, his frail grip on the saddle horn could never have held him in place. Guiding the pinto was impossible. He had no choice but to rely on the surefooted mountain savvy of the beast.

They skidded through the gravel, and the pinto took off with a bound. Falling as much as running, the horse dived down the slope in a series of gut-shaking leaps. For the first time real pain stabbed along Glen's side and brought a red tinge to his vision. With each jarring impact, the pain stabbed deeper.

The foot of the grade was rushing up at them. Glen felt a terrible certainty that the pinto could never survive the impact. Horse and man would be dashed into broken carcasses when they hit bottom. He closed his eyes just as the pinto kicked off with his thrusting hind legs and hurled himself outward to plummet the last fifteen feet.

All four legs buckled at the impact, and the sturdy horse lurched awkwardly sidewise. Glen's head whiplashed on his neck, but he still heard the distinctive rush of air past his head. A bullet! Somewhere up above them Quirt had been waiting for the instant when they landed to try for a shot. He had come close but the pinto's stagger had made him miss. And, Glen could tell by the sound of the bullet's passage, they were getting near to the limit of even Quirt's range.

The pinto caught his balance. Glen could spare the noble beast no time to rest. He drummed his heels against its ribs and gave a hoarse yell that sent the pinto lunging forward. Glen reeled in the saddle. Empty grassland stretched before them. He fought to force back the scarlet-tinged darkness that threatened to submerge his mind.

With bound hands he shifted the reins first right then left, putting the pinto into a zigzag course. The horse was panting, foam flying from his mouth, but he raced gamely on.

Glen's senses dimmed. He didn't know if Quirt had fired again. The pain savaged his side like a burning brand. He felt himself sag forward. Quirt had beaten him, he thought with his last fragments of awareness. The bushwhacker had claimed another victim. Limply he sprawled into darkness.

Chapter Seven

"Sis! Sis, come here quick!"

Barbara Turner stiffened at the urgency—panic?—in her brother's voice. Dropping the rolling pin she had been using to flatten a malleable lump of bread dough, she dashed from the kitchen into the hallway that led to the front. Automatically, she used her apron to wipe the flour from her hands as she moved.

Her father's old revolver was hanging in its holster on the coat tree in the foyer. As she had on other occasions, she hauled the big pistol free before going out the door.

She had not been expecting Peter—Pete as he liked to be called—back so soon this afternoon. He had seen to his chores before heading over to Glen's place to check on the livestock there.

Glen. Thinking of their neighbor by his first name had come easily to her. Peter had already spoken of him in glowing terms before his fortuitous appearance in backing down Jason Rathers a few days before.

But it had been more than her brother's friendship with the quiet rugged rancher that had led her to think of him in such intimate terms, she had been forced to admit blushingly to herself. Glen Douglas had stirred her heart and touched her secret longing in a fashion no man ever had before, a fashion she'd come to fear was impossible for her.

Perhaps, she had half believed, the romantic thrills she had longingly read of, or heard her friends gushingly describe, were not meant for her. Oh, there had been some suitors, but they had been no more than faces and names, and none of them had been the sort of man she would ever consider as a serious beau.

But Glen was such a man. She had known it from their very first meeting. His taciturn ways, masculine strength, and awkward kindness had captivated her thoroughly. Indeed, so strong had been the attraction she felt that she'd had trouble forcing herself to behave in a properly modest fashion around him.

Did he have any such feelings for her? The question never seemed to quite leaver her mind. She believed he did. Yesterday, there in town before he had ridden out to hunt down the killer no one else could catch, she was sure she had read in his eyes a yearning to take her in his arms. Had he done so, even in broad daylight on the public street, she knew she would not have resisted.

But the moment had slipped away, and she had let him go with so much unsaid that she wished to say. The thought of him riding coolly and confidently up into the hills after the killer had burdened her cruelly, stretching her nerves as taut as the barbed wire some of the ranchers were starting to use.

Heavy gun sagging in her fist, she burst now out of the house and froze in shock at the scene before her. Peter was struggling to loosen some kind of ties holding a slumping figure on a black and white horse that was terribly familiar. The roan mare Peter had been riding when he left the homeplace stood to one side, snorting and pawing at the ground in excitement. Ranger, their hound, was dancing about.

"Help me, Sis! It's Glen! I think he's been shot!"

Panic stilled her heart, but she moved reflexively to lay the gun aside on one of the porch chairs and rush down the steps. As she reached them, Peter finally got the reins unknotted. Glen slid loosely from the saddle almost into his arms. Peter staggered beneath the weight. Barbara lent her own strength to the effort, and together they eased him to the ground.

The pinto dropped an inquisitive nose toward his master. Glen's face was pale, his features slack. Barbara felt her chest contract as she saw him.

"Is he—" she gasped.

"He's alive," Peter cut her off.

Barbara nodded curtly. She could cope with an injured Glen. The other alternative had been unthinkable.

"His horse came limping in to his place with him tied on like you saw him," Peter rushed to explain. "I figured I better just bring him here."

"Yes, of course." Barbara didn't look up from where she knelt beside Glen's still form. She couldn't tell how badly he was hurt. The pinto's muzzle came probing down once more. Impatiently she shooed the animal away. "Let's get him in the house," she urged Peter.

He moved swiftly to help her. Clumsily, with Glen's weight suspended between them, they mounted the steps and toted him into the house.

"Put him in Dad's room," Barbara said, panting. She could hardly bear to let her eyes rest on Glen's waxen face.

At last they got him sprawled on the bed. Gingerly Barbara fingered the strip of sacking bound around him. She would need scissors to cut it away, she realized.

"I'll go fetch the doc!" Pete volunteered.

"Okay." Barbara didn't look up from her ministrations. Then, as she heard Peter's steps nearing the door, she turned sharply. "Peter."

He paused, glancing back over his shoulder.

"Hurry," she said with soft urgency.

Peter nodded. Yeah.

Barbara heard his rapid exit from the house. Quickly she heated water and used it to moisten the strip of burlap. It was crusted with dried blood, but, she was thankful to note, there didn't seem to be any fresh bleeding.

Although her volunteer work in the hospital back in Kansas had prepared her a bit for this task, she still felt woefully inadequate. But she knew that it would be a good spell before Peter could get back from Davis with the doctor. Her own efforts might mean the difference between life and death for Glen.

Carefully she used the scissors to snip through the sacking before peeling it back. Next his shirt had to be cut away. She felt herself flushing at undertaking this intimate task. Unbidden, the image of him standing shirtless beside his corral flashed across her mind. Angrily she put such distractions aside and concentrated on the task at hand. Now wasn't the time for romantic fantasies *or* false modesty.

Glen mumbled and shifted beneath her touch. She took it as a good sign, but noticed the growing crimson hue of his features. She pressed a palm to his forehead, then drew it back. His temperature was climbing; she was certain he was coming down with a fever.

Despair touched her. There was so much to do, and she felt helpless before the magnitude of the task. Pausing in her efforts, she took time to kneel by the bed and pray.

When Peter did return with the doctor, Barbara had

her patient clad in the bottoms of a pair of her father's long johns. She had cleaned the ugly wound as best she could, bound it, and laid a cool cloth on Glen's fevered forehead. To her, Glen seemed much more relaxed and comfortable than earlier.

Dr. Willard Tomley examined her handiwork closely, having to undo some of it to inspect the patient. She had met him at church. He was young and unmarried, and the admiring look he gave her made her avert her eyes.

"You did all this?" he prompted.

"How is he, Doc?" Peter cut in impatiently.

The physician seemed a little perturbed at having his conversation with Barbara interrupted. "He could be a lot worse," he announced. "Apparently a bullet—a large one—glanced off his ribcage and kept going. He's got two busted ribs. From what you tell me of the way he rode in, I'd say it's a minor miracle his lungs or other organs weren't punctured by those ribs. He's lost some blood, and he's got a fever. It's not a good idea for him to be up and around until those ribs are stronger, and he'll need tending for some time."

"Oh, I can do that!" Barbara volunteered so eagerly that both men gaped at her in surprise.

"Well, I mean it would be convenient since he's already here, she managed to stammer.

Young Dr. Tomley glanced at Glen's supine form, then back at her. She fancied she could read disappointment in his eyes. Peter's sly grin made her furious. She was thankful when Tomley turned back to the bed.

When the doctor was finished, he gave Barbara some final instructions and said that he would stop back by later in the week. He appeared disheartened at her reserved response.

"I'll go see to the chores," Peter said once Tomley was gone. "It's too late to head back over to Glen's place. I'll do that in the morning, first thing."

Barbara nodded. She had neglected her own household duties, and hadn't even started yet on dinner.

Along with fried ham and cornbread for herself and Peter, she fixed a thin broth with the intention of spooning some of it to Glen after dinner. But he was sleeping comfortably, and she decided it was best to let him rest.

For a moment she stood over him, gazing at his face. Then she reached down and drew a tender hand across his forehead. His fever was definitely lower, and she let her fingers linger.

Catching herself, she withdrew her hand. There was still work to do. She bustled back to the kitchen to finish the dinner dishes.

She was arranging a pillow and blanket in a rocking chair next to her patient's bed when Peter peered in inquiringly. "What are you doing, Sis?"

"I thought I'd stay in here tonight," she said defensively, "In case he wakes up or needs something."

She expected some sort of teasing gibe in response,

and steeled herself to receive it. But Peter just nodded slowly. "Good idea." He smiled at her and she felt a rush of warmth for him.

"Night, Sis."

"Good night . . . Pete."

His smile turned into a grin, and he disappeared. She could follow the sounds of his footsteps down the hall to his room.

In her own quarters she changed into a long night-gown and pinned her hair back before donning a robe and returning to the sickroom. She lowered the lamp's flame to a mere flicker, and positioned the rocking chair to give her a clear view of her charge. She was careful to be sure the door was ajar.

She knelt to say her prayers before settling comfortably into the rocker. Even under the innocent circumstances, she thought drowsily just before sleep claimed her, there was something pleasant and comforting about sleeping here in the same room with Glen.

She dozed off and on through the night, awakening often to check on him. His condition appeared unchanged, except once she awoke and imagined she felt his eyes on her. But when she rose and went to his bedside his eyes were closed, and his breathing was deep and regular.

Glen slept on through the breakfast she prepared for herself and Pete before sunrise. Pete rode out shortly afterward to return to Glen's spread and finish the chores there.

Barbara washed the breakfast dishes and checked
on her patient. Although his fever seemed to have broken, he still slumbered soundly. A twinge of concern
touched her. How long was he going to sleep? Deter-
minedly she put her worries aside and went to see
about her household tasks. Glen was suffering from a
bullet wound, shock, and fever, she told herself. Sleep
was healthy for him. He would awaken when his body
had recovered more of its strength.

Still, she couldn't resist peeking in at him occasion-
ally as she cleaned the house. Churning the butter
came next. Finished with that, she was preparing to
go outside and see to the hens when she heard Ranger
give his warning bay. Cautiously she peered out. Her
heart lurched in her breast.

Jason Rathers, clad in what looked to be his
Sunday-go-to-meeting best, was just climbing down
from a glossy black carriage. Puzzled, Barbara cast her
eyes right and left, but the ranch owner was alone.
None of his hard cases had accompanied him.

Her heart was going at a gallop now. What could
Rathers want? She thought of Glen, lying helpless
abed, and she recalled the suspicions he had voiced
about Rathers. Could Rathers intend harm to Glen? At
all costs she must protect her patient.

Rathers had just started toward the house when she
emerged. He faltered in his step, then halted and
smiled engagingly at her from under his full mustache.
The smile slipped a little when he caught sight of the
revolver she held leveled in her fist.

"No need for that," he advised. "I'm here to make peace and apologize."

She couldn't hide her startlement, but she wasn't ready to trust him any further than she could throw their roan mare.

"Your apology is accepted," she replied coldly. "Good day."

His smile widened with a hint of amusement. "Honestly, Barbara—" He broke off. "May I call you that?"

"I'd rather you didn't," she said, not yielding an inch.

He sighed with the air of a man unjustly wronged. "Very well, but I'm not here to upset you or cause trouble."

Barbara wished fervently that Pete would return. She questioned silently whether Rathers had somehow known he was absent. "What do you really want?"

Rathers spread his hands in a conciliatory gesture. "Like I said, to make amends. I think maybe we've gotten off on the wrong foot, and I'd like to try to change that. I'm not that bad of a fellow, or a friend, when you get to know me." Again came the engaging flash of his smile.

Barbara sensed suddenly that the aging rancher fancied himself a ladies' man. In his younger years he might've been quite handsome and dashing. He was trying to use some of that stale charm on her now. She wanted to shudder. It was like having a snake slither over her.

"There's nothing that needs changing," she told him firmly. "And I've no desire to get to know you any better. We've told you where we stand. This place isn't for sale."

"If you'd just give me a chance—" he began, and advanced a step as he spoke.

She shoved the barrel of the pistol forward a couple of inches and he halted. "Now you wouldn't really use that, would you?" he jeered.

"You're trespassing. I've asked you to leave. I've got a right to use it." Somehow she kept her voice level.

Rathers studied her. Whatever he saw apparently kept him standing where he was. For the first time Barbara detected a hint of anger in his countenance. His nostrils flared, and his smile grew thinner.

"I believe if we sat down like reasonable civilized people and talked this over, we could reach some sort of arrangement," he started again. "You're a lovely young woman. Surely you don't want to spend your life working like some sharecropper on this two-bit spread. The sun and labor will turn you old and haggard before your time. You belong at fine restaurants and elegant dances—"

"I belong right here."

Rathers fell into a frustrated silence. He looked past her at the house. "How's your patient?" he asked without warning.

Surprise rippled through her. How had he known

Glen was here? she asked herself, then recalled the doctor. Or maybe Rathers was having their place watched. Word of Glen's presence would've been certain to have reached Rathers eventually, she realized.

And if Glen's suspicions were sound, her mind raced on unbidden, then Rathers might've learned that Glen had been shot by the bushwhacker himself. She could feel her face go pale at the thought. If Rathers was capable of hiring a cold-blooded murderer, what would he be willing to do to her right now, if he was of a mind? The pistol suddenly seemed small and ineffectual in her grasp.

"I'd like to see Douglas if he's available," Rathers went on companionably, but Barbara knew he had somehow scented her fear.

"I can't help you," she said stubbornly.

"I think maybe you can." Rathers started toward her once again.

"You looking for me, Rathers?" Glen's voice sounded coolly from behind her.

Barbara turned her head sharply. Glen stood in the doorway, fully dressed, even to having donned one of her father's shirts. He looked wan and shaky, but his gunbelt was nonetheless strapped around his lean waist. Stepping past her, he faced Rathers squarely.

Rathers froze in his advance. Shock showed on his face. Then his eyes narrowed as he assessed the man standing before him. "You're not looking well, Douglas."

"I'm well enough to settle any business we might have." Glen crooked his arm just a little, so his gun hand was poised. Barbara's breath caught at the determined gleam in his eyes.

Looking at Rathers, she felt a thrill of fear. The rancher brushed back his coattail to reveal the butt of his pearl-handled gun. He stood tense and ready as well. Could a weakened Glen outdraw the older man? she wondered fearfully.

"What about it, Rathers?" Glen prodded, somehow finding the strength to stand even straighter. "You and I can settle this right now and put an end to all the killings."

Barbara felt her body go taut at his naked challenge. She bit into her lower lip so hard it hurt. The faces of both men seemed cast from the unyielding limestone of the Arbuckles.

Then Rathers relaxed a fractional bit. "I'm not sure I savvy what you mean, Douglas."

"You savvy it all right."

"No, I don't," Rathers protested. "I wanted to see if you'd reconsidered my offer."

"I never considered it in the first place. Now get off this land, or make your play." Glen was trembling ever so slightly, Barbara saw. She prayed Rathers couldn't detect it.

The face of the rancher shed the last vestiges of its charm. "I'll be going then," he growled. "And I'll give you both a piece of advice: Watch your backs;

the bushwhacker's still at large.'' Pivoting on his heel, he strode to the carriage.

Barbara reached to lay a soft hand on Glen's shoulder. Whether it was an effort to lend him strength, or merely a gesture of affection, she didn't know. Perhaps it was both. Beneath her palm she could feel the tremors racing over him. He seemed to be standing by sheer will alone.

Rathers drove away without looking around at them. Glen stood where he was until the conveyance was some hundred yards distant. Then he turned leadenly toward Barbara, opened his mouth as if to speak, and slumped in collapse at her feet.

Chapter Eight

Glen became aware of the touch of a cool palm on his forehead. He opened his eyes and found himself gazing up at the pretty features of Barbara Turner.

"Oh, you're awake," she exclaimed, almost snatching her hand away.

"Where's Rathers?" Glen managed to ask as memory came back to him.

"He's gone," Barbara assured him. "How did you ever get on your feet and come out there like that?"

"I was worried when I woke up and heard his voice through the window," Glen brushed the question aside. "How long ago was that?"

"A little over two hours."

Glen shifted in the bed and realized the shirt he'd appropriated had been removed. He still wore his

Levi's. Tentatively he touched the bandage at his side.
It was fresh.

"You started bleeding some when you collapsed on
the porch," Barbara explained. "I managed to get you
back in bed and rebandage the wound." A flush
touched her face as she spoke.

"How did I get here in the first place? I just recollect passing out on my horse."

He listened as she described the events of the past
two days. "You've been nursing me the whole time?"
he said when she finished.

The flush in her cheeks deepened. "Yes."

"I'm obliged."

"The doctor said you're not to get up and about
until your ribs have a chance to heal." She appeared
eager to get past the subject of her caring for him.

"I don't want to be a burden. I'll go back over to
my place and rest up there."

"You'll do no such thing," she told him firmly,
then blushed even more.

The notion of staying here with her tending him was
a pleasant one, Glen decided. His side ached like a
mule had landed both hind feet there, and he felt weak
as a pup. He wasn't disposed to argue with her. "I'll
be beholden to you," he said sincerely.

Barbara's face lit up at his surrender. "You've done
so much for us, this is the least we can do. But you
must be hungry and thirsty. I'll rustle up something
for you." She turned toward the door.

"Where's Pete?" Glen's query stopped her.

"He's out checking on the stock. He'll be in shortly."

Glen nodded. She bustled out, and he let himself relax in the softness of the bed. Barbara's image lingered in his mind, but a bleak assessment of his man-hunting efforts quickly dispelled it.

Quirt had got him cold. If he hadn't caught on to the drygulcher's ploy in that last half second, he would've joined the ranks of Quirt's victims. His Winchester had been no match for Quirt's bushwhacker's gun. The completeness of his defeat rankled him.

He was still brooding when Barbara returned with a bowl of soup, a chunk of cornbread, and a mug of water.

"Do you need me to feed you?" she asked earnestly, holding the tray primly before her.

Glen's desire to be babied by her only stretched so far. "I can manage," he said gruffly.

"Oh." She looked disappointed. "I'll just leave it then."

"No, stay here," Glen requested quickly. Fretting about what happened wasn't going to help matters any, and the company of this girl would do him good. Anyway, he needed some answers.

Sitting with his back propped against the headboard, he drank thirstily, then spooned the soup down. He nibbled at the cornbread. The simple fare was about all his belly was up to for the moment. Perched on the foot of the bed, Barbara chattered as he ate, filling in details of the past two days that her earlier account had omitted. She finished by describing the arrival of Rathers.

"I've never been so happy to see anyone as I was to see you standing there!"

"You're still not interested in selling to Rathers?" Glen probed.

"No, of course not!" she answered with some surprise. "Why would you think we were?"

He shrugged. "You're putting yourselves in some danger."

"This place was Dad's dream," she told him intently. "He was a storekeeper up in Kansas, but he'd worked as a cowboy when he was young, and he always wanted a ranch of his own. I can remember him talking about it when I was just a little girl. Her eyes were distant. "When Mother died, I was almost grown, and Dad figured Pete was old enough to make a good hand. Dad had heard about how you could lease land cheap from the Indians, so he sold the store and came down to negotiate a lease. He used most of the money to buy cattle to start the herd. Pete came with him."

"You got left behind?"

She nodded a bit wistfully. "I wanted to come; I didn't have anything—or anyone—to hold me in Kansas." Her eyes caught his for a moment. "But Dad decided this was no place for a woman just yet. He said it was dangerous, and, besides, there were no beaus for a young woman down here.''

"He might have been wrong about that last part."

She looked down quickly, but he thought she was pleased. "Anyway," she went on, "he and Pete left me with my aunt and uncle up in Kansas. I was to join them when they had things running. Dad had written me saying it would just be a couple of more months. I got the letter only two days before I learned of . . . what happened.'' Her white teeth pressed against her lower lip.

"And you came down to help Pete," Glen added.

"Yes, that's right. It took awhile to arrange things. My aunt and uncle didn't want me to come. They offered to let me stay with them. But I knew Dad wouldn't have wanted this place to be lost. It meant too much to him. And I knew Pete couldn't handle it all by himself. I've never regretted coming."

She was pioneer stock, Glen mused. Strong and faithful, she was the kind of woman who'd make a man a good wife and bear him sturdy sons and virtuous daughters.

She became flustered under his gaze. "Pete told me you used to be a deputy marshal."

"For a spell," Glen conceded.

"What made you settle down to be a rancher?"

Glen hadn't told too many people the story of his last manhunt as a lawman. But Barbara needed to be told. She was attentive to his words, shuddering at his description of the ruthless killing of the outlaws.

"Quirt sounds like an awful man," she opined.

"He's the bushwhacker."

"What?" she gasped.

"I ran into him in the mountains. He all but admitted he was doing the killings because someone was paying him. He's the one who shot me."

"That's terrible," she breathed. "Now that you know who it is, can't you go to the marshal?"

"Nothing's changed," Glen told her. "Manning would never find Quirt unless Quirt wanted to be found. And then it'd just be Manning's bad luck that he did find him."

"But Quirt's only one man."

"He's not like any other man I've ever known," Glen told her honestly. "I think he kills just for the sake of it. And nobody's better than him with a long gun."

Drowsiness was abruptly settling over Glen. He blinked and shook his head. Barbara caught the movement. "Oh, you need to sleep."

"You were in here last night, weren't you?" Glen asked groggily. "I remember seeing you in the chair."

"Here, I'll take the tray. You rest." She bent over him, and he was dimly aware of her warm feminine presence and the sweet, flowery scent of her. He struggled to keep his eyes open.

"Let me put the pillow behind your head." He felt the touch of her hands as she adjusted the pillow and the bedclothing.

Those were his last impressions before sliding down into slumber.

When he awoke he lay still for a time, gathering impressions. From the flickering lamp and the pale gray light outside the window he could tell it was dusk. Somewhere nearby a cow lowed. He'd slept away most of the afternoon, he realized with irritation.

He was alone. There was no sign of his pretty nurse, though pleasant memories of her lingered.

Gingerly he laid the covers aside, thankful to see that he was still in his Levi's. He sat up, wincing at the pain in his taped and bandaged side, and swung his legs off the bed. For a moment the room rocked and nausea surged in him. He clenced the blanket tightly in his fists until the sensations passed.

Disgusted at his own weakness, he pushed himself slowly up onto his feet. His legs wobbled beneath him, and he caught the bedpost for support. He didn't doubt his need for rest and recuperation, but the quicker he got up and about, he reasoned, the quicker he would regain his strength.

A wave of weakness made him question his conclusion. But stubbornly he gathered himself and let go of the bedpost. He was like a newborn colt still trying to get its legs under it, he reflected darkly.

Hand outstretched in front of him for balance, he took one tottering step, then another. As he tensed himself for the third, Barbara appeared in the doorway, an armful of linens clasped to her breast. She gasped in surprise at seeing him on his feet. Startled, Glen recoiled, and felt his balance go. As he began to fall, Barbara dropped her load of linens and sprang forward to catch him.

He had an instant's sensation of her softness and the brush of her hair before he felt himself supported with surprising strength. Not resisting, he let her help him back to the bed. He was panting, and sweat was beaded on his bare chest. He was a lot worse off than he'd thought, he concluded bleakly. His earlier exertions hadn't been nearly so trying.

"What ever did you think you were doing?" Barbara chided.

Glen shook his head ruefully. "Trying my legs again. I guess it was a little early."

"I should think so." Barbara eased him firmly back onto the bed.

Glen managed a weak grin as she straightened. "Sorry for all the bother. It's not often I need a nursemaid." he studied her briefly, then added, "You make a mighty pretty one."

"Flattery won't get you any leniency in this hospital." She was clearly happy with the remark. She pointed an emphatic finger at him. "Now, you have to promise to stay in bed until the doctor has come to see you again."

"I promise," he said, then tacked on, "for now."

She gave him a mock scowl that faded into a look of genuine concern. "It's no joking matter. The doctor said another inch or two, and the bullet would've killed you for certain.''

Glen remembered the jolting impact of the big .50-caliber bullet glancing off his ribcage. He repressed a shudder. A mere graze by Quirt's buffalo gun was almost as serious as a direct hit by a small-caliber weapon.

A thought prodded him, and he twisted his head to look about the room.

''If you're searching for this, it's right here at hand.'' She indicated his gunbelt hanging on the head-board. Its presence was reassuring to Glen. He made a mental note to check it over when he was alone.

''Where's Pete?'' he asked.

''Outside finishing the chores.'' She bent to retrieve the discarded linens. ''I was just putting up the wash before I start dinner. Looks like I'll need to keep a closer eye on you.''

''My pleasure,'' Glen told her, then sobered. ''When Pete comes in, I'd like to see him.''

''Good. He's been badgering me about you ever since he got back. I told him you needed your rest, and that he wasn't to bother you.''

''It's no bother.''

When she left, the room seemed duller and drabber. Glen was relaxing comfortably when he heard booted footsteps in the hall. Pete Turner's sturdy figure appeared in the doorway.

''I told you I should've gone with you,'' he reminded Glen immediately. "We could've gotten him in a cross fire."

"Not this hombre," Glen assured him.

"Who was he? Did you get a look at him?"

Glen described the events of his abortive manhunt. Pete listened raptly. "Golly, he must be good!" he exclaimed when Glen finished.

"Maybe the best," Glen agreed quietly.

Pete stared at him soberly. "Then how can he be beat?"

"I got the drop on him once," Glen recalled aloud. "This time he got it on me. That makes us even."

"Can you do it again?"

"I'm not sure," Glen admitted. "Right now, I couldn't get the drop on an Eastern tenderfoot."

"You sent Rathers hightailing this afternoon," Pete pointed out. "Barbara told me all about it."

"Rathers isn't Quirt."

"But Barbara said you think Rathers is behind the killings. Why not just go after him?"

"There's no proof Rathers is responsible," Glen said. "And don't go repeating my suspicions around. That's a good way to get yourself in trouble, unless I miss my guess. I can't touch Rathers without proof, or unless he makes some play himself. He may be too smart to do that. He was today. He'll let men like Quirt and Reno do his killing for him."

Pete began to pace impatiently back and forth. He smacked a solid fist into his palm. "We've got to do something!"

Glen appraised him shrewdly. Young, impetuous, and frustrated, Pete was trouble waiting to happen. "Listen to me, Pete," he ordered. "Don't go off half-cocked. Quirt's a pro at what he does. You're an amateur. That's taking nothing away from you. It's just speaking the truth."

"Well, what are we going to do?" Pete demanded. "We can't just sit here like bumps on a log!"

"I'm going to rest up and get my strength back," Glen said evenly. "I'll still need you to keep an eye on my place. Can you do it?"

Pete halted his pacing. "Sure I can. But—"

"And I need you to do one more thing," Glen said to cut him off. He fumbled in the drawer of the bedside table and found a scrap of paper and the stub of a pencil. Awkwardly, propped on one elbow, he scribbled on the paper.

"You know Blake Sedgeman, the gunsmith in Davis?" he asked when he was finished.

"Yeah," Pete answered with some puzzlement. "I know him."

"Tomorrow I want you to go into town and see Sedgeman. Give him this, and tell him to make the order by express freight. He can put it on my account. Understand?"

Pete nodded.

"Here." Glen extended the scrap of paper.

Pete took it and read the words printed on it. His eyes widened.

"Tell Sedgeman this is all confidential," Glen went on. "And you keep quiet about it too, even with your sister. Got that straight?"

"I've got it!" Pete assured him. "I'll see it's taken care of." He turned and hurried from the room.

Glen lay back on the bed. Now he had some waiting to do.

Chapter Nine

From where he sat on the Turner porch, Glen recognized the thin slump-shouldered figure of Oscar Manning well before the marshal reined his gray up in front of the house.

The lawman crossed his wrists on the saddle pommel and let his shoulders sag forward even farther. "You're up and about, I see," he remarked by way of greeting.

"Up, anyway," Glen temporized. "The doc says I've still got a spell before I'm fit for much of anything."

Manning grunted. "I heard you was out here. I figured it was about time I made it over to check on you."

The marshal had taken his own sweet time, Glen

reflected dryly, but he didn't speak the thought aloud. "I'll be headed back to my place in a couple of more days," he said instead. "I imagine Barbara and Pete will be glad to be shed of me."

In truth though, he doubted it. Barbara, in particular, appeared to glean much pleasure and satisfaction from her nursing duties. And Glen found himself slow-footed when it came to giving up her care for him.

But there was still a job to be done. . . .

"Where are Pete and Barbara now?" Manning glanced about the homeplace.

"They went into town after supplies." Enjoyment of this easy living aside, Glen knew he'd been a burden to the determined pair. He put the thought aside. "Light down,' he invited the marshal.

Manning did so with a grunt of effort. He mounted the steps and took the other ladder-back chair beside Glen. "The Committee was mighty sorry to hear what happened," he said.

"Tell them I'm obliged for their concern."

"Reckon it was a mistake to ask you to do a thing like that," Manning opined.

"Looks that way, don't it?"

Manning regarded him from tired gray eyes. "You ain't going back to try for him again?"

Glen shifted uncomfortably against the hard wood of his chair. "Would you?"

"Nope," Manning admitted readily enough. "But I thought you might."

Glen stared into the distance. "He hit me from nigh onto nine hundred yards. Grace of God I'm sitting here at all."

Manning nodded heavily. "I reckon I understand. I'll pass it on to the Committee."

"Give them my regards."

After the marshal rode out, Glen stayed on the porch. Ranger kept him company. His strength was slowly returning. The wound had healed, and his ribs were mending. Still, he knew it would be a long time before they would be as good as new. Too long. He felt the pressure of passing time. But to act before he was ready might just get him killed. Besides, he reminded himself, he still wasn't outfitted properly.

When the buckboard hove into sight in the distance, Glen pushed himself out of the chair and onto his feet. He couldn't help wincing at the twinge from his ribs. He leaned against one of the uprights and waited.

Barbara had worn a yellow dress and sunbonnet for the trip to town. She made a pretty picture sitting up on the wagon seat alongside her brother, Glen thought. He was having such thoughts a lot lately.

Over Barbara's protests, Glen insisted on helping tote the bundles and sacks of supplies into the house. He was careful not to do any wincing under her watchful gaze. When they finished, Pete caught his eye and Glen accompanied him to the barn to unhitch the mule.

"We passed the marshal back down the road aways," the youth informed him as he loosened the traces. "He said you told him you weren't going after the bushwhacker again.'

"That's what I told him," Glen confirmed.

"Then why did you have me—" Pete began.

"No need noising my plans about to the marshal," Glen cut him off in a drawl.

"Yeah. Well, I stopped by and saw Mr. Sedgeman. He said your order came in yesterday. He ain't told nobody about it."

Glen felt an instinctive flexing of the muscles of his shoulders. "In that case, I'll ride into town tomorrow and pick it up. Figure it's about time I moved back out to my place as well."

"Barbara won't be happy," Pete said. Something in his tone said he would miss Glen's presence around their homestead himself.

"She's been expecting it," Glen told him.

Pete nodded and fiddled restlessly with the harness.

"Are you sure you need to go after the bushwhacker again? There haven't been any more killings since you were shot."

"He's waiting for me," Glen said.

"What?"

"He knows he didn't kill me, and he knows that, when I'm able, I'll come after him again. But he can't be certain when that will be. If he drygulches another victim, then he might give me a starting place to track him. He's too canny to do that."

mused, but the name didn't fit. The only sport the big rifle was suited to was that of killing.

It fit awkwardly in his saddle sheath as he rode to a remote corner of his spread. A gunnysack of empty tin cans dangled from the saddle. He chose a flat barren area where erosion had washed away the topsoil so no grass would grow. On foot, with the pinto tied in a grove of cottonwoods, he set the cans up at regular intervals; one hundred yards, two hundred, three hundred, until he had placed all of them. He had to set the last one on a fence post so he would be able to see it at all. It was a long hike back to the starting point.

The sun was hot and yellow in a sky flecked with white clouds. The wind out of the west was steady, but didn't amount to much by Indian Territory standards. It carried the scents of dust, sage, and buffalo grass. Glen used his field glasses to scan the surrounding country side. He spotted a few head of his cattle grazing in the wind-rippled grass to the east. A pair of coyotes capered on a far-off ridge. Other than that, he saw no sign of life. No mounted figures broke the roll of the prairie.

The Arbuckles were distant dim shapes, almost like gray storm clouds building on the horizon. Glen had the sudden unsettling notion that hostile eyes were gazing on him from the mountains even at this impossible distance. He shook the feeling off.

Opening a box of shells, he knelt and thumbed the

"You sound like you know exactly how he thinks."

"I do, up to a point."

Pete swallowed and nodded. His eyes were wide.

As her brother had expected, Barbara objected to Glen riding a horse, to his leaving her care, and to his returning to his own place.

Glen was unyielding, and at last she consented with a sigh. He saw the disappointment hovering in her tourquoise eyes, and wanted to say something reassuring. But there was a growing eagerness in him to reach town and, once more, take matters into his own hands. Hollow words would be a waste of breath.

He rode out on the pinto, gratified to find that straddling a horse wasn't the ordeal he had feared. Nonetheless, he held his mount to a walk over the distance to Davis.

He fancied he felt curious eyes on him as he guided the pinto into town. He kept a watch for Rathers and any of his crew, but none of them appeared to be around.

The gunshop of Blake Sedgeman was on a side street at the edge of town. The frame building housed a small showroom in front and the workshop and living quarters in back. Behind the shop was a long narrow lot that served as a firing range to test the merchandise. A wall of hay bales made a backdrop for the targets.

The front door stood open. When Glen used the screen door a bell announced his presence. In a handful of seconds Sedgeman emerged from the workshop. His dark face—usually woeful—split into a grin as he saw his customer.

"You've come for it, have you?" he said in greeting. "I knew you wouldn't be able to wait once I got word to you. Stay here." He disappeared in back, then returned, reverently bearing an object wrapped in oilcloth in his arms. Moving behind his counter he laid his burden gently on the glass surface. Deftly he undid the bindings, then looked up with a smile to catch Glen's reaction as he flipped the cloth back.

The rifle revealed bore a superficial resemblance to Glen's Winchester. But it was longer, the bore wider and octagonal in shape. Oil gleamed sleekly on its metal surfaces.

Glen stood gazing at it and barely heard Sedgeman's voice reciting a litany of praise. "Just like you ordered. First one I've ever seen, and I'm sure not disappointed. Winchester 1886 Sporting Rifle, lever-action, 50-110 express, eight-shot magazine, outfitted for a telescopic sight, and fitted with a special-order thirty-inch barrel. You like it?"

Glen nodded almost absently. He reached out and picked up the huge rifle, hefting it thoughtfully. He worked the lever once to be sure the magazine was empty. The mechanism functioned with smooth precision. Swinging away from the gunsmith, he lifted the piece and settled the brass plate of the walnut butt firmly against his shoulder. The sight at the end of the barrel seemed a long ways off.

He lowered it, lifted it again more quickly. At al most eight pounds, the Sporting Rifle was heavier tha he was accustomed to in a long gun, but its balanc made it easy to handle.

Reluctantly he laid the rifle back on the counter, h gaze lingering on its gleaming finish. He'd have to du that some, he reflected. Too easy for it to catch th sunlight and cast a betraying gleam. How would shoot? he wondered. He looked up to meet Sedg man's expectant gaze. The gunsmith passed him th scope sight to examine.

At length Glen nodded. "I'll take the whole outf Add in all the ammo you ordered."

Sedgeman grinned, then grew serious. "Good lu with it," he said seriously. "I haven't told anybo about it, and I won't start now."

Glen nodded his thanks. He settled up, then cover the metallic menace of the Sporting Rifle in the c cloth once more. With it tucked under his arm, exited the shop. He bound the gun to his saddle a left town by a back route.

Although he kept the pinto to a walk, his side h a twinge to it by the time he reached his place. P had done a good enough job of caretaking, he no absently, but there were still plenty of odds and ei he would need to see to as soon as possible.

But for now he had another chore. In the house, cleaned the Sporting Rifle carefully, removing all the factory grease. The weapon was a marvel,

big cartridge into the magazine. A lot of powder and lead here, he reflected. Rising, he worked the lever, settled the big rifle against his shoulder, and sighted carefully on the nearest can. He didn't expect a hit on the first shot. Even with a top-notch weapon, a man had to get to know it before he could expect much accuracy with it. Still, he took his time. When the shot felt right, he squeezed the trigger.

The brass shod butt slammed his shoulder, and thunder crashed in the sky. Glen felt a twist of pain in his wounded left side. A hundred yards in front of him, the can ceased to exist.

A little stunned, Glen tramped to the site to confirm his hit. His eyes hadn't fooled him. Only splinters and fragments of tin remained. He rubbed his shoulder and headed back to the firing line.

At two hundred yards he raised a miniature explosion of dust and gravel with his first shot. On his second, the can once again disappeared. If his target had been a man standing upright, even his miss would've been a killing shot. He clenched his teeth as he remembered the shocking force of just a graze by Quirt's Sharps.

As the range increased, he used the pinto to check the results of his shots. He was pleased with the big gun's performance.

He was riding back from the six-hundred-yard target when he spotted another rider bearing down on him. He dismounted at the firing line and waited for Barbara Turner to reach him. She wore the same divided riding skirt in which she had been clad on that other visit she'd made to his place. He had no doubt the sound of the shooting had draw her here.

She pulled rein and looked down at him; her pretty features were pensive. "I made Pete tell me what was going on," she said by way of explanation. "He told me about the new rifle. I had to come see you."

"You know you're welcome here," Glen told her.

She acknowledged his words with only a scant dip of her head. "You're going after him again, aren't you? That's why you ordered the rifle."

Glen nodded affirmation. "Yes."

She didn't dismount, as though what needed to be said required some space between them. "He might kill you this time."

Glen hitched his shoulders in a shrug. The weight of the rifle seemed to drag at his arm. "Me or somebody else," he agreed. "He'll kill again. Maybe I can stop him."

She leaned toward him, and her loveliness was compelling. "I can't talk you out of this, can I?" she implored.

Glen shook his head. "You shouldn't try," he said quietly.

Briefly she bit her lip, then she straightened in the saddle. "I know," she admitted in a sigh.

Glen watched her and felt an ache deep in his chest.

"Promise me one thing," she urged.

Glen waited.

"Tell me before you leave. Please?"

"I'll tell you."

She looked as though she meant to say more. But her blue eyes grew cloudy, and she wheeled her mare sharply about.

Glen stood unmoving until she was out of sight. Slowly he raised the heavy rifle once more to his shoulder.

For the final two cans he used the scope. It brought the targets into startling clarity.

The day was long when he dismounted by the fence post where he'd set the most distant can. He had used up a box of shells. His shoulder and side ached. His ears rang, and the smell of powdersmoke filled his nostrils. He surveyed the results of his last shot, then drew a deep breath of satisfaction and looked down at the weapon in his hands.

The Sporting Rifle was everything he'd wanted. In caliber and range it was the virtual equal of Quirt's Sharps. And its eight-round magazine meant it didn't have to be reloaded after each shot.

Glen raised his eyes toward the distant mountains where Quirt waited. His fists tightened about the rifle. Now he had his own bushwhacker's gun.

Chapter Ten

Dusk was gathering when Glen rode up to the Turner homestead and dismounted. Barbara met him at the door. Her evident pleasure at his coming faded as she took in the drab range clothing that he wore, the gear on his horse, and the hard set of his features.

"You're going, aren't you?" she whispered.

Glen gave a nod. "I promised I'd tell you when I did."

She slipped out of the house and pulled the door shut behind her. She stood very close in the gloom of the porch. He could see her pale face tilted up to gaze intently into his.

"Are you well enough to do this?" she asked.

"My ribs are fine. I'm ready."

"How long will you be gone?"

"Until I get him."

She swayed toward him, her lips parted as if to speak.

Gently Glen pressed a finger to those soft lips. "No," he told her. "We'll talk when I get back."

"What if you don't get back?"

"Then all the talking we do now won't make any difference."

"Yes, it will," she insisted. "To me."

Glen studied her for a long moment. "Then I'll tell you this," he said hoarsely. "I love you. There's no other woman for me besides you."

"And I love you, Glen." She barely breathed the words.

Glen folded her in his arms and pressed his mouth to her waiting lips. She strained against him, and it was some time before they drew apart.

"I'll be waiting for you," she promised softly. "Come back to me."

"Yes," Glen said.

He released her and turned away. Going down the steps, he mounted the pinto. He took one last look at her pale figure in the shadows of the porch. Then he wheeled the horse and put its nose toward the Arbuckles.

The prairie stretched away into darkness. Deliberately he had chosen a moonless night. This time Quirt wouldn't see him coming.

The rolling grassland seemed to reveal itself to him in stages as he rode. The ground that fell away beneath his horse's hooves disappeared into the darkness behind him. The day's heat had lingered. It clung oppressively to man and beast alike.

At last the stars in the night sky ahead of him were blotted out by the upthrusting mass of the Arbuckles. He skirted a field of successive ridges of rock, all leaning in the same direction at an identical angle, like waves frozen in stone.

He slowed the pinto to a walk. A solid black wall appeared to loom ahead of him. It was a thick covering of pine trees on a steep slope, and he threaded the pinto in among the fragrant trunks. He could feel the horse's muscles bunch and play as the grade steepened.

Halfway up the face of the mountain, he cut into a rocky defile he remembered of old. On foot, testing each step for loose stones, he led the pinto deeper into the remote fastness of the range. Finally, with the pinto hobbled some distance away, he slid under an overhang and waited for dawn.

Between catnaps he chewed on the task that awaited him. As he knew from experience, the Arbuckles made a mighty big region in which to locate one man, particularly a man who didn't want to be found, and who knew these stunted mountains, if anything, better than Glen himself.

But Quirt had been living the life of a recluse up here for a good spell now—maybe for years. He could survive off the land, with ammunition and luxuries such as coffee and tobacco presumably supplied by infrequent contact with a cohort (Rathers?) on the outside. Likely he would have a number of dens and hidey-holes, but he was almost certain to have main sanctuary—a hide-out—that was his center of operations.

Such a haven would be secluded, its entrance possibly concealed from the casual eye. Some of these mountains were like anthills, with caves and tunnels snaking through their depths into regions never seen by the eye of man. It would be in one of these caves where Quirt would live, Glen reasoned.

And the other requirement Quirt would need for his life as a murderous hermit would be a lookout point from which he could view his surroundings and spot interlopers into his domain. That spot would be atop one of the tallest peaks in the mountains. In fact, Glen concluded as he mulled it over, Quirt would probably have several such vantage points. His hideout would be close to one of them. Glen recalled a number of peaks that would fit the bill.

Dawn found him up and moving. He'd had a cold breakfast; he wouldn't risk a fire until he was sure it was safe. On foot, staying to cover, he worked his way toward the highest peak within sight. He'd had occasion to skirt its base in the past, but had never scaled it. It had all the earmarks of the sort of spot Quirt would use as a lookout.

The going was slow. Glen had to negotiate steep grades, narrow defiles, and tangled underbrush. Always he was haunted by the awareness that Quirt, at any moment, might be drawing a bead on him with the Sharps. He'd never know what hit him, Glen reflected darkly. Quirt would hide his body, and he would become one more mystery of these benighted peaks.

He shrugged the unnerving thought aside, pausing to rig a sling for the Sporting Rifle. It would be harder for him to bring it into play, but he needed both hands to climb.

Often sheer cliff faces or dead-end draws made him double back. He found a game trail that he recalled of old, and stayed on it gratefully for a little ways. He was aware that he was more exposed here, but the surrounding rocks and trees gave him some cover. He studied the trail closely, but there was no sign of other human passage.

When he left the trail he entered a draw splitting the side of the mountain that was his goal. The draw looked to reach all the way to the summit. Its floor was a jungle of stone and brush. He moved cautiously upward through it, pausing at times to scan his surroundings with his field glasses.

He flushed a white-tailed deer from a thicket. It bounded agilely away across the rocks, tail flicking like a banner, and disappeared in the trees lining the rim of the draw. Glen frowned. That dancing tail could be seen a long ways by an experienced eye, and spooked game was a dead giveaway that something else alive and dangerous—maybe a man—was in the area. Glen changed position and stayed put for a little while, but he saw no sign that he'd been spotted.

He labored on, scrambling and pulling himself over and around the huge rocks. The sun shone into the defile and he felt its hot pressure on his neck and back. The stone walls trapped the heat. Later in the day, the nooks and crannies of the defile would become ovens.

At length he reached the wooded summit of the mount. He skulked through the trees, the heavy weight of the Sporting Rifle in his fists now. He found several spots that made good lookouts and spent some minutes at each, using his field glasses much as he imagined Quirt did from time to time. He was deep in the mountains. Their hunched, rugged shapes spread out in all directions. The rolling grassland of the plains seemed only a distant, impossible memory.

He could find no sign of Quirt on the summit. Frustration nudged him, but he knew it was too early in the hunt to hope for results. The fact that Quirt hadn't left traces of his presence did not mean that he didn't use the summit as a vantage point from time to time. Glen would simply have to keep searching.

His legs were feeling the strain of the climb. With his back against a convenient boulder, he rested, chewing on jerky and using his field glasses. He was careful to shade their lenses from the sun, which was high overhead now. The betraying reflection from a lens would make a fine target for Quirt if he happened to spot it.

The glasses showed him no evidence of other human life, although he did pick out another likely peak that might serve as a lookout post.

Lifting the glasses a bit, he detected what appeared to be heavy storm clouds building far off in the west. He imagined the summer storm racing across the prairie, such as he had often witnessed. By late afternoon the Arbuckles might be in for some rain. Glen scowled at the prospect. A downpour would erase any signs of Quirt's recent comings and goings and make travel in the mountains a sight more difficult.

Glen surveyed the other likely lookout station once more, then stored the field glasses and headed in that direction.

He reached it by midafternoon, and found himself in a region of the mountains with which he was unfamiliar. A man could spend years in these broken lands and still not know all their ways and passages.

Ascending the peak consisted of catching the thin trunks of dense stunted trees and pulling himself up the steep grade, his feet scrambling for purchase. Where possible he bypassed the dense thickets that sometimes clung to the slope beneath the trees. Visibility was poor in the shade, but he kept his eyes peeled for another human figure moving among the trunks. The need for constant watchfulness would, he knew, start to wear on him after a time.

He began a careful survey of the mountaintop, finding only two sites that made for decent observation points. It was at the second of these—a rocky ledge overlooking a sheer drop—that he went to one knee to peer closely at a brown stain on the stone. It was dry, but it was not old.

Bending close, he sniffed, and his nose wrinkled at the acrid scent of stale tobacco juice.

Glen rocked back on his heels in satisfaction. Quirt wouldn't risk cigarettes for fear the smoke or the flare of a match might betray his position to a watcher. But, kneeling here, with a chaw of tobacco in his mouth, he had spit carelessly off the edge. Some of the juice had spattered on the stone.

Searching, Glen found other signs that this ledge saw frequent occupation. There was no layer of dust on the ledge, nor was there the usual accumulation of twigs, gravel, and debris he would've expected to find. The view of the surrounding terrain was outstanding. Plainly Quirt used this spot regularly.

When he came back, Glen could be waiting for him.

It was a good strategy, Glen decided. He would have to find someplace to conceal himself, and then bide his time. He looked about him for a likely hiding place.

A single shot sent echoes bouncing off the forested peaks.

Instinctively Glen ducked, then realized that the shot had not been meant for him. Somewhere, he surmised, Quirt had been hunting for game to fill his larder, and had made his kill. The deep boom of the Sharps was unmistakable.

What direction had the shot come from?

Glen listened to the dying echoes and looked for powdersmoke, but saw none. The shot hadn't been close, and the up-and-down geography made it hard to estimate the source.

At last Glen settled on a wooded valley partially concealed behind the shoulder of a mountain to his west. He debated only a few moments. He could always come back here to wait in ambush, but, for the nonce, he needed to push on toward the likely location of his prey.

He had to skirt the mountain in order to descend. Then he wasted no time in making for the valley. He traveled a bit faster than was safe, exposing himself recklessly on occasion, spurred by the need to reach the valley before Quirt left it. Still, the terrain didn't allow for very rapid travel in the best of circumstances.

The afternoon was nearing its end, and the storm clouds—black and ominous—were looming close when he crested the ridge overlooking the valley. He paused to reconnoiter. Below him was a sea of pines. A cool breeze, sharp with ozone, suddenly rushed across the ridge. It was the forerunner, he knew, of the oncoming storm.

He looked toward the cloud bank. It bulked huge and dark above the mountains, like a giant over pygmies. The entire western sky was blotted out. Thin yellow blades of lightning darted earthward from the clouds, and thunder rumbled in their heart. For a moment Glen stood awed by the sweep and scope of the storm's power.

He shook the reverie off. He needed to get moving down into the valley. He took a step forward and something whipcracked up past his ear with a shock of displaced air that knocked his head to one side. Rolling over the distant thunder came the boom of the Sharps.

Glen ducked and flung himself flat. His nerves raced frantically. Quirt! Somewhere down below, the bushwhacker had seen his carelessly exposed figure and fired on reflex. Glen's single step forward had made him miss, but, even so, not by much.

With a convulsive twist Glen shrugged the Sporting Rifle off his back and brought it around. But he had no target. The trees below and served to dispel any betraying smoke. Another shot gouged upward through the dirt in front of him. Glen returned fire by guess and instinct, then wriggled backward off the ridge. He couldn't afford to stay here where Quirt already knew his precise location. His answering shot had been only to let the bounty hunter know he was still alive and kicking.

Quirt would be coming after him, but he wouldn't be doing it rashly, and when he reached the crest of the ridge, he would probably think his quarry had retreated straight down its far side. Instead, Glen worked his way about a hundred yards along the ridge, just below its crest. Then, behind an outcropping of boulders, he pulled up to wait.

Had Quirt recognized him? Glen had to figure that such was the case. It meant Quirt would know he was up against a seasoned and dangerous adversary.

The rolling black wall of the storm was rushing toward him. Before long, Glen mused, he and Quirt would be stalking one another through these mountains in a harsh driving rain. He peered down the barrel of the big Winchester and waited.

Minutes limped by like the box turtles that dwelled on the forest floor. A few cold drops of rain splattered down. Glen could actually see the wall of rain advancing in his direction a couple of mountains away.

Quirt should've crested the ridge by now, he calculated. The fact that he hadn't could only mean he had employed some other strategy than what Glen had expected.

Time to pull up stakes, Glen decided. He'd been long enough in one place. Too long, he understood an instant later as a shot roared and an explosion of shards erupted from the boulder that concealed him. Quirt had somehow spotted him again.

Glen stabbed a return shot at the barely glimpsed muzzle flash of the Sharps, then crayfished backward. He went plunging down the slope. Quirt had him on the run. He tamped down the panic that threatened to claim his legs. His best bet was to take cover in the broken tangle of rock at the bottom of the deep draw below.

The storm hit as he raced down the slope toward shelter.

Chapter Eleven

The storm came with a bludgeoning fury. Almost instantaneously the rain changed from scattered drops to a blinding deluge riding on the teeth of a battering, pummeling wind. Glen almost lost his balance beneath the first impact. Lightning struck close enough to shake the ground beneath his feet and fill his vision with a brilliant flare. The thunderclap slammed against his ears. He reeled into the shelter of a leaning slab of stone.

Rock chipped near his face, and it took a heartbeat to realize a bullet had once more come close. Deafened by the thunder, he hadn't even heard the shot. Again, even in the rain, Quirt had targeted him. Glen retreated. Quirt had the high ground, and now, with the storm raging, was no time for a showdown.

Abruptly the ground right in front of his boots disappeared. Desperately he threw out his arms for balance, stiffening his legs and digging in his heels. The weight of the rifle in one outflung fist almost overbalanced him. For an awful clocktick of time he teetered on the brink of the drop that had been invisible in the driving rain. Then he caught himself. His jaw tightened in grim dismay at what he saw.

Before him, and stretching away to either side, was a sheer drop that looked to be all of sixty feet. If he hadn't seen it in time he would've gone plummeting off to smash into the stony floor of the draw.

He sleeved water from his face and flung a look over his shoulder. He could see only the rain falling in rippling sheets. But he knew Quirt was back there somewhere, and he knew he didn't have time to look for an alternate route down into the draw.

Slinging the big rifle, he turned, dropped to his knees, and let himself over the edge. At every instant he expected to feel the devastating shock of a .50-caliber shell slamming into him. It would be the last thing he ever felt.

One downward straining leg found sparse purchase, then the toe of his other boot settled into an unseen niche. With a gasp of relief he ducked below the lip of the drop. But he wasn't safe. He was clinging by fingers and toes to rain-slickened rock three score feet above the floor of the draw. The rain lashed at him, threatening to tear him loose by its sheer force. The wind howled, and he felt its power seek to pluck him from his precarious perch.

Falteringly, he inched one leg farther down. The sole of his boot slipped off wet stone. No purchase there. He kicked against the face of the cliff; his boot slid, then caught on a tiny ledge. He couldn't take the time to test it. He trusted his weight to it and lowered his body with straining arms.

A wet rock knob gave him a grip for his left hand. The fingers of his right clawed their way into a tiny fissure. He repeated the whole procedure with legs stretching blindly below. Thankfully the cliff face was rough and uneven, providing uncertain hand- and foot-holds. But the rain all but blinded him. Of needs, he must proceed by feel and instinct and prayer.

Lightning crashed somewhere nearby, and the stone shivered beneath his fingers. Inch by inch he groped his way downward. Somewhere above, Quirt would be working his way toward the lip of the cliff. The driving rain, his own hunter's caution, and perhaps puzzlement over his prey's disappearance would slow him, but he would be coming just the same.

Glancing up, Glen thought for one heart-gripping instant that he saw the killer's shadowy figure already silhouetted atop the cliff, sighting contemptuously down along the enormous barrel of the Sharps. Then realization came to him that it was only a trick of the rain and wind and light—and his own fevered imagination. But the shock of the apparition rippled through him nonetheless, setting his muscles to trembling. One foot slid from its scant toehold, and rock crumbled beneath his other boot. For a second's eternity of time he fancied he hung by fingernails and sheer will. The wind whipped at him, catching at the rifle on his back. Far from being his salvation, its awkward weight might overbalance him and pull him to his doom.

Then one scrabbling foot caught on a bulge of rock, easing the strain on his arms. He pressed himself against the stone face. He knew he must keep going, but the effort to move his frozen muscles was even greater than what he'd already exerted. At last he extended a shaky leg one more time.

By clawed hand and braced foot, he descended. How long had he clung and crawled like an outsize rock lizard? He dared to snatch a glance earthward. A breath of surprise tore at his lungs. The floor of the draw lay only about ten feet below him.

Relief made his muscles go slack. He sensed himself falling that last short distance, and tried to twist to protect the rifle. He got one leg under him, but the impact buckled it and sent him sprawling on his side. Pain jolted through him, and with it a stab of fear that he'd recracked his ribs.

He made it up on one knee and from there thrust himself to his feet. He was panting harshly, and he sucked the cool rain into his mouth. His first step was an awkward lurch. Then the muscles of his legs tightened to support his weight.

His strength began to filter back as he headed into the stone wasteland choking the floor of the draw. He knew he could be in a death trap if the rain caused a flash flood to sweep through the gully. But getting clear of Quirt's rifle was what mattered most right now.

He clambered out of the rocks into another, narrower draw that branched off at an angle from the main fissure. Staying near one smooth stone wall, he followed the new course as the rain continued to pound at him and the thunder rumbled overhead.

He was fairly certain he had shaken Quirt. Still, after a spell, he took the precaution of unslinging his rifle and waiting behind a bulge in the rock wall to see if he had a follower. He was soaked to the bone, and he thought ruefully of the slicker cached with his saddle and other gear.

Nothing appeared on his backtrail. He moved on, casting wary eyes upward at the rim of the draw for possible danger, and for a way to higher ground. He needed shelter now; he had stayed long enough in the draw. In the heights behind him, rivulets would be joining to form streams, which would merge into yet larger flows, until muddy torrents rushed down the canyons and guillies, carrying everything before them.

But the walls of this draw remained sheer and unbroken. Wet, they were too slippery to scale. They offered none of the handholds he had used in his earlier descent.

Glen increased his pace, hurrying now. The rain lashed at him, obscuring his vision even beneath the brim of his Stetson. Errant gusts of wind tore through the draw. Gloom closed about him as if it were dusk.

And then, behind him, even above the cacophony of the rain, he heard the mounting roar he'd dreaded. He began to run, not looking back. He knew all too well what was at his heels. The berserk elements themselves might do Quirt's job for him.

Breath rasped in his lungs, and he choked as he drew in air and found it almost half water. He stumbled over something unseen, held his balance with a painful twist of his body, and managed to catch his stride again. To his rear the roar increased until he imagined a locomotive bearing down on him. But here there was no way to get off the tracks.

His rain-blurred vision almost missed it. An opening gaped in the wall a yard above his head. He slid to a stop, turned, and flung himself upward. His reaching hands fell short of the lip of the black maw.

He gathered himself to spring again. As he did, from the edge of his vision he caught a nightmare glimpse of a wall of water a dozen feet high rushing down the draw upon him. Borne in its teeth were logs and debris and some kind of dead animal.

He jumped, straining upward with every muscle in his body. His clawing hands grasped the lip. He heaved himself up and into the opening in a single surge. But he was still too low, still too vulnerable.

When it passed, the flash flood would fill this niche as well.

He scrambled forward, then spotted some kind of gap above him. He snaked himself through the narrow hole and clambered upward in near darkness. Rocks tore at his hands. The rifle slung on his back clattered against stone.

A rushing sound tore past beneath him. Water lapped at his feet, and for a moment he felt the tug of it. Then he was safely above it, collapsing on some sort of ledge in semidarkness.

For a pair of minutes he lay there, panting, offering up a worldless prayer of thanks. A few feet below him, water splashed and gurgled.

At last he rolled over and sat up. He peered about his sanctuary in the dimness, casting his eyes upward.

The bony fanged head of a dragon leered down at him.

Glen recoiled, fumbling frantically for his rifle. Then he froze in astonishment as he comprehended what he beheld. Embedded in a natural stone wall before him was the gigantic long-necked skeleton of what he took to be some kind of ancient seagoing beast. Parts were missing, but he could plainly discern the snarling fanged head as large as his torso; the snaky vertebrae of the neck; the enormous ribcage; and the short tail. One handlike forelimb was clearly visible. He estimated its length at forty feet.

Overawed, Glen rose to his feet. What eons-old cataclysm had imprisoned this monstrous beast here? He'd seen fossil shells scattered in these mountains, but never observed anything the likes of this find. Once, untold ages ago, these mountains must've been under water, submerged in some prehistoric sea in which monsters of this sort swam and hunted.

He turned his head to survey further. For the first time he realized he was out of the rain, although the drumming of its fall still echoed from without. His mad scramble had taken him into a sort of cave formed by collapsed and overlapping layers of stone. Some ancient upheaval had created a tomb for the gigantic fossil beast, protecting it from the elements and exposure. He shook his head in mute wonder.

There was nothing to do but wait for the water to subside. He explored briefly. The cavern did not extend far. He found evidence of animals having made lair there from time to time, but little else. He pondered how long it had been, if ever, since human eyes had gazed on the fantastic sight of the entombed beast.

With some scraps of wood in the cave, he built a fire, then settled down, grateful for the dryness and warmth. The smoke would dissipate before it made its way outside.

His latest encounter with Quirt had turned into another near disaster, he mused bleakly. Once the storm had struck, neither of them had had much of a chance. But his final assessment was grim. Now Quirt knew he was in the mountains. And if his foe's ear was as good as he suspected, the boom of the Sporting Rifle had told Quirt that he wasn't the only one armed with a heavy-gauge weapon. Now Quirt would be hunting for him, just as he stalked Quirt.

The muted beating of the rain slackened. Bestirring himself, Glen crossed to the rim of the ledge. The water was receding from the niche that had given him access to the cavern. Returning to the fire, he kicked it out, then slung his rifle and eased down into the niche.

The water lapped near the tops of his boot as he waded out and looked into the draw. A dwindling river of muddy brown water still ran there. He hunkered down and waited a spell longer. Finally, he unslung the rifle and dropped into the shallow water, crouching as his legs flexed to take the impact.

With caution, he traveled downstream. Debris of varied sorts had been piled along the base of the rock walls. A low spot allowed him to scramble from the draw. He made his way out of the forest of stone and headed warily back toward the valley where he had located Quirt.

Only a few drops of rain were falling now, although a cloud cover hung overhead. Off to the west he could see the edge of the cloud bank. The sun had sunk low enough to shine straight in under it. The golden beams caught the moisture in the air and cast every color of the wooden mountains in brilliant unnatural clarity. The green of the pines shone with a blinding emerald hue.

He could see nothing of import when he reached the ridge over the valley. Concern about the hobbled pinto prodded him. In the fading brilliance he worked his way back cross-country to the spot where he'd left the horse. Drenched and bedraggled, but otherwise unharmed, the pinto snorted his displeasure with his master. Glen's saddle and other gear, concealed beneath his tarp, were dry.

Glen relocated the horse and equipment to another spot a good ways distant. It was dark by the time he rubbed the animal down, and then once more left it hobbled in a secluded mountain park.

He put some distance between himself and the horse before settling in the shelter of a rocky outcropping. He dared not risk a fire, but his exertions had dried out his clothing for the most part. Largely by feel in the poor light, he cleaned the rifle and his revolver thoroughly. After a meal of salted ham and canned peaches he settled into his bedroll. In his dreams the ancient sea dragon came writhing out of the darkness to snap at him with fanged jaws.

Morning found him working the kinks out of aching muscles and joints as he returned to the pinto. All looked to be secure and he left the steed grazing contentedly and in much better spirits than the night before. Having the pinto in the mountains was a burden of sorts. However, the time might come when the animal would be invaluable to him. But for now he could move with greater stealth and freedom on foot.

He spent the day in a fruitless crisscrossing of the valley that Quirt had made his hunting ground on the day just past. The rain had destroyed any trace the bounty hunter might've left but Glen had been hoping Quirt would return to search for him.

Near the end of the day, he found himself wondering wryly if Quirt might not have spent the daylight hours searching through the barren jungle of stone for him.

Tired and frustrated, his nerves frayed raw, he returned to the mountain park where he'd left the pinto. After a careful circuit of the area to be sure an ambush wasn't awaiting him, he moved the horse yet again. The hobbled pinto might make easy prey for one of the pumas that prowled these mountains, but the risk was one he had to take. Hopefully the big cats would look for easier prey that didn't carry the dreaded odor of man.

He was tempted to return to the cavern of the fossil beast, but the dangers of using the same sanctuary twice were too great. Instead, he found another lair and turned in for the night. For a time he lay on his back staring up into the darkness, his head propped on his arms. He could tramp these mountains for years looking for Quirt, he calculated sourly. More than likely he would end up blundering into Quirt's sights as he had almost done already. Better to let Quirt come under the barrel of the Sporting Rifle if he could manage it. With that conclusion in mind, he slept.

In the first hours of the morning he once more scaled the mountain where he'd found Quirt's lookout point. His earlier reasoning was still sound. Quirt was currently operating out of this area. If he was patient, and used Quirt's own observation point, he just might be able to draw a bead on the bounty hunter before he fell victim to a bushwhacking himself.

The morning haze was still on the forest blow. He settled in on the high ledge and unslung the Sporting Rifle. Deftly he attached the scope and used it to sight in on a few spots below him. Satisfied, he set the rifle aside and unlimbered his field glasses. A ridge of stone offered a prop for his elbows. He lifted the glasses to his eyes and twirled the gauge to focus them.

Movement flicked in the brush far below him.

It came and went so fast he wasn't sure he had seen it. He pressed the glasses tighter to his eyes, hunching forward as he sought to catch sight of the figure he had glimpsed. But no other movement caught his eye. He swung the glasses in a slow arc, gripping them so hard his knuckles ached.

Setting them aside, he snatched up the Sporting Rifle and used its scope. His hands flexed with the automatic impulse to lever the big Winchester and throw lead down into the wooded gorge, but he reined in the impulse. Firing blind would be a greenhorn's play.

At last he lowered the long gun. His teeth ground together in frustration. He was certain he had just glimpsed the buckskinned figure of Quirt sliding through the early morning haze like a wraith. But as quickly as he had seen the bounty hunter, he had lost him.

For long minutes he waited, but only an easygoing coyote trotted into view. At sight of it, Glen relaxed disgustedly. The animal's unconcerned presence told him that nothing human was nearby. Quirt had slipped away.

Glen pondered. No doubt Quirt was setting out to stalk him. Had he himself been a little quicker, Glen thought darkly, the whole ugly contest might be over. But self-recriminations would do him no good. Providence had given him an edge; he knew where Quirt had just been. And, more importantly, he knew the area and direction from which Quirt had come. Chasing Quirt was risky business, he had already decided. But waiting for him was another matter.

His pulse quickening, Glen left the lookout point and headed down the mountainside. He moved rapidly, certain that Quirt wasn't lurking nearby. Pausing on occasion, he kept the spot where he had seen Quirt pinpointed. By the time he reached it, he was sweating and out of breath.

He crouched in the brush for a spell, watching, listening, scenting the breeze that rustled through the trees. He detected nothing to alarm him. Reassured, he fell to examining the ground.

Only a faint scuffed place in the carpet of fallen leaves and pine needles betrayed Quirt's trail. Frowning in puzzlement, Glen glanced about. Where had Quirt come from? A steep limestone bank covered with a thick growth of vines was before him, and there was no trace of anything having descended it. Not even Quirt could have come down its sheer face without disturbing the tangled mass of vines.

Then the odd darkness behind a section of the growth made him bend forward to peer more intently. He picked up a broken branch to probe through the vines. He felt it scrape against stone, then abruptly his arm straightened as the stick failed to meet further resistance. In a single smooth movement Glen dropped the branch and palmed his Colt. He used his left hand to reach out and grasp a fistful of the vines. Warily he eased them aside and found himself staring into the black mouth of a cave that angled down toward the stone heart of the mountain. The rock floor of the cave mouth was scuffed clear of dust by the regular passage of feet.

Glen sucked in air through gritted teeth, then exhaled it in a slow sigh of satisfaction. A hunter's instinct told him he had found his prey's den—Quirt's hideout.

Chapter Twelve

"I'm back, Sis," Pete announced, then broke off. "Oh, sorry—didn't mean to disturb you."

"No, that's all right, Pete." Barbara rose from where she'd knelt in prayer at her bedside. "I'll fix dinner in a minute. I was just praying . . . for him."

"Yeah," Pete spoke gruffly. "Been doing some of that myself."

He was still in his work clothes, Barbara noted absently. It was late in the afternoon, and he must've just come in from doing his chores. Earlier, as he'd done for the past few days, he'd ridden over to Glen's spread to look after things there.

"It's been four days," she heard herself murmur.

"Don't worry." Pete stepped awkwardly toward

her, then halted. "He'll be back. He can take care of that Quirt fellow."

His tone wasn't as confident as she knew he wanted it to be, but his clumsy efforts at reassurance touched her heart.

"I know he'll be back, Pete," she told him softly. "It's just hard waiting like this, not knowing. . . . "

"You care for him, don't you?" His voice was serious, with none of the teasing note it so often carried.

Barbara started to answer, then had to bite her lip and squeeze her eyes almost closed to stop the tears that suddenly wanted to spring forth. She nodded mutely.

"I admire him near as much as I did Dad," Pete confessed. He hesitated, then added, "I think Dad would've like him."

"I think so too," Barbara said when she found her voice.

There was a moment of awkward silence between them. *We've known each other as children,* Barbara thought suddenly. *Now we've got to get to know each other as adults.*

"See you in the morning, Sis." Pete turned toward the door.

Ranger's abrupt, strident baying sounded from outside.

Both of them stiffened. Barbara felt her heart go into a gallop. Something in the pitch of the dog's voice told her that he was trying to warn them of a lot more than a varmint sniffing around the henhouse.

"What is it?" she gasped.

"Stay here," Pete ordered tersely. "I'll go see."

Before he could move, the glass in her bedroom window shattered, the sound lost in the crash of a shot.

"Get down!" Pete yelled. He lunged to grab her and press her to the floor, kneeling beside her.

More shots came. Barbara heard glass breaking elsewhere in the house. Men's voices shouted harshly. The pounding of horses' hooves vibrated like drumbeats.

Staying low, Pete scrambled to the window. On hands and knees, Barbara followed. She felt broken glass cut into her knee through the fabric of her long dress. She raised up behind Pete, putting her hands on his shoulders. His muscles were tense and hard beneath his shirt. She looked past him and out the window, already guessing what she would see.

Mounted men, pistols spitting flame in their fists, were racing around the house like renegade Indians of old. Barbaric yells had taken the place of war whoops, but the bloodthirsty savagery was every bit as real. Barbara ducked as a bullet struck splinters from the window frame.

"I'll get the shotgun!" Pete exclaimed. "You stay here and keep low!"

"No!" Barbara cried. "This is my home too. I'll fight for it!"

Pete didn't argue. She followed his crouching retreat to the front of the house. The shotgun leaned against the wall by the door. Next to it was Glen's rifle, which he had left with them when he'd bought his new one from the gunsmith. Pete snatched their father's gunbelt from the coat tree and strapped it around his waist. He picked up the shotgun, broke it to check the loads, then dropped to a knee beside one of the front windows. He used the barrel to knock out the remaining shards of glass left by an attacker's bullet.

He had to wait only an instant before one of the riders swept in front of the window, some twenty yards out. Pete muttered to himself and touched off both barrels.

Barbara shuddered at the roar in the confinement of the room. She saw the horse and rider both go down in a sprawl of flailing limbs.

"Now they'll know the Turners don't roll over for anybody!" Pete exalted. He broke the shotgun to reload.

Coughing from the powdersmoke, Barbara reached for the rifle. "I'll go to the back!" she managed.

Pete nodded wordlessly. He crammed in two more loads.

Barbara hurried through the house, pausing to grab a box of shells from the hall cabinet. The shouting and gunfire had slackened a little with Pete's hit, but she knew in her heart that their attackers wouldn't give up this easily. They had waited until Glen was gone—dead? she wondered fearfully—and then pressed home their ruthless designs.

The kitchen windows offered the best view of the rear of the house, but she was also more exposed there. Ducking, she hurried to the nearest one nevertheless, and crouched to peer out. A trio of riders had halted about seventy-five yards distant and seemed to be conferring. Others were galloping this way and that, still throwing some shots. She ignored the latter, concentrating on the three talking things over. Anger flared in her as she recognized the rugged frame of the ramrod, Reno, on the center horse. Where was Rathers? she questioned silently. Had he accompanied his men on their dirty job?

A little clumsily she worked the Winchester's lever, jacking a shell into the chamber. She hadn't done much shooting in her life, but her father had seen to it that she knew how it was done. From the front of the house came the boom of Pete's shotgun, followed a moment afterward by a second blast.

Barbara lifted the rifle and sighted. She'd never shot at another human being, but rage at this violation of her home steeled her arms. She pulled the trigger, felt the painful jolt against her shoulder as powdersmoke obscured her vision. Blinking through it, she saw the three riders scattering. With mingled regret and relief she realized she'd missed all three of them. But the bullet must've come close.

Furiously she worked the rifle's lever. It was easier this time; her movements were more confident. She fired again, then once more, still not scoring any hits. The fast-moving riders made elusive targets.

Suddenly a fusillade of bullets tore at the window frame and whistled past her head. She dropped flat with a little cry of surprise. They had spotted her and were returning fire. On her stomach she wriggled across the floor and rose up in front of the twin iron sinks. They offered her some protection as she peered out the window behind them. She still had no idea how many of the attackers there were. A good dozen, she guessed. Rathers must've used his whole crew of hard cases for the raid.

Bullets still tore at the window she'd just vacated. As she looked for a likely target she saw one of the riders starting a run straight for the window where they must still believe her to be pinned down. Rifle to his shoulder, reins in his teeth like some Wild West Show performer, he came charging, levering and firing as he came. Plainly, he was to administer the coup de grâce.

Barbara lifted her own rifle. A dreadful calmness settled over her. The horseman came thundering in. Her rifle barrel tracked him at an angle. She refused to look at his face, only at his centaur form as he drew nearer. Just before he would have to swerve to avoid piling full tilt into the side of the house, she squeezed the trigger.

She had a horrible image of him slewing sideways out of the saddle before she swung her head sharply away, her eyes tightly closed. She couldn't tell if the pounding in her ears came from the gunfire or the throb of her racing pulse.

She looked again after only a pair of seconds. Her target—victim—lay sprawled on the ground. His horse was bolting away. Over the thudding in her brain she heard a chorus of angry yells. She ducked for cover behind the sinks as lead came her way again. A bullet *spanged* off one sink in an ugly whining ricochet.

But the barrage didn't last. It tapered off quickly as though orders were being given. She waited tensely, the rifle gripped hard in her fists. After a moment, the ruckus from in front of the house quieted as well. Carefully she edged her head up.

Riders were trotting back and forth. But they had pulled away to where, while they probably weren't beyond the range of a good rifleman, they were certainly beyond her limited abilities. What was going on? Were they getting ready to give up and ride out?

"Hello the house!" the hatefully familiar voice rang out as if to answer her questions. Jason Rathers was here, all right.

Where was the rancher? Barbara swung her head frantically back and forth, rising up farther for a better view. But their nemesis was not in sight. She guessed he must be invisible to Pete as well, or she would've heard the boom of the shotgun.

"You okay, Sis?" Pete's voice bounced through the house.

"Yes," she quavered, then raised her voice to repeat herself, "Yes! I . . . I got one!"

"Good!" Pete sounded savage. "Can you see Rathers?"

"No, no I can't!"

Silence fell.

"Come on!" Rathers shouted from his place of concealment. "I know you can hear me. There's no need for this killing. We can settle things peaceable!"

"You're the man who came with the guns!" Pete hollered back suddenly. Barbara felt a thrill of pride that his voice showed only determination.

"And I've still got plenty of guns left, if need be, to finish the job!" Rathers countered.

"You'll need every one of them! And you still won't get it done!"

"That's mighty big talk, boy!" Anger overrode some of the sham reasonableness in the voice of Rathers.

"It's more than talk!"

Another silence descended, as though Rathers was trying to get himself under control. "Hear me out!" he shouted then.

"I'm listening."

Barbara had almost forgotten the lurking riders, caught up as she was in the tension of the exchange. She forced herself to remain watchful as she listened to the shouted conversation.

"This can all be over with if you and your sis want to come out and talk business. My offer to buy your outfit still stands."

"I done told you! We ain't interested in selling!"

"You got no choice, boy!"

"This shotgun says different!"

Barbara felt another surge of pride at Pete's courage. It faded as she heard the outraged voice of Rathers calling again.

"Hang it, Turner, this was just supposed to be a hoorawing! There wasn't to be no bloodshed! Now you done gone and killed two of my hands! I can't just let that lay!"

"Your men came shooting. "Don't blame us for shooting back! Ride out before you lose any more of them!"

"Can't do it!" Rathers bellowed harshly. "If you won't sign over your outfit, my boys are going to want blood. You understand me?"

Barbara's throat was dry. Her ribcage seemed suddenly to tighten about her heart.

"I reckon I understand," Pete called after a handful of seconds. For the first time, his voice sounded hoarse and strained. "But let my sister come out! There's no call for her getting hurt!"

Barbara heard her own startled gasp. Forgetting caution, she sprang to her feet and dashed back through the house. Pete had changed positions to another window in the parlor.

"No!" she exclaimed. "I won't leave you!"

Rathers cut off any reply Pete might've made. "Afraid that's not in the cards," came the rancher's voice.

"You lousy backshooter!" Pete screamed. "What kind of man are you?"

"One who gets what he wants. Now, I'll let you and your pretty sister both go, if you'll take my offer. Deal?"

Pete turned an anguished face toward her. "Sis—"

"Pete, he'll kill us both if we go out there," she cut him off. "He's intended to from the beginning! Can't you see that? Our only chance is to fight them."

"We won't win. There's too many of them. And I don't want anything to happen to you."

A bullet tore over Pete's head and went by Barbara so closely she felt its heat on her arm. Caught up by her emotions, she'd carelessly remained standing in plain view of the window.

'Watch out! Pete dived to pull her to the floor, but she had already flung herself prone.

"There!" she gasped fiercely. "Do you see what I mean?"

Pete nodded wordlessly; his eyes were desperate. Turning, he scrambled to regain his place at the window as the gunfire opened up again in earnest. Barbara heard the thud of bullets from outside. But Pete and her father had built the house well. Its sturdy walls were thick enough to turn most shells.

Pete heaved up and cut loose with the shotgun. Dropping it, he pulled the six-gun and snapped a shot.

Barbara scurried back to her vantage point in the kitchen. She was none too soon, she saw as she raised up to look out. Three men on foot, having apparently abandoned their horses in favor of stealth, were creeping rapidly toward the house from widely divergent angles. Drawn guns gleamed in their fists.

Barbara didn't stop to think. The men were too close, the danger too imminent to allow for anything but automatic reaction. She jerked up her rifle and threw a shot at the man on her left. Not waiting to see the results, she swiveled the rifle, cocking it as she did so. The center hard case came in line with the barrel, and she fired again. She was only barely aware of the kick of the rifle butt against her shoulder. Squinting through the smoke, she completed the swinging arc of the rifle barrel and fired a third time at the remaining man. Only then did she pause to see the results of her fusillade.

The first man was beating a hasty retreat. The second had dropped to the ground, but didn't appear to be hit. The third gunman was the least rattled. Crouched, he was extending his cocked pistol and aiming carefully for her window.

Barbara flung the rifle to her shoulder and fired first. She sensed immediately she'd acted too fast to have any sort of accuracy, but the bullet must've zipped close by her target, for he flinched wildly. Then, lowering his pistol unfired, he whirled and took to his heels.

Barbara kept shooting, driving all three to cover. They began to pepper the house with their six-guns.

Barbara had to duck away and move to another window. With clumsy fingers she reloaded. Cordite seared her nostrils and burned her eyes. She heard a yelling rider gallop close past the house, but by the time she raised up her gun, he had disappeared around the corner.

"Let me show you young 'uns a taste of what you'll get if you don't give this nonsense up!" Barbara cringed at Rathers's muffled voice.

The gunfire from outside faded to a halt. A slow minute dragged past. Barbara waited, afraid to risk taking a look. She realized her breath was coming in short gasps, and she made herself breathe more slowly.

Pete's shogun boomed, jolting her with surprise.

"Sis! You better come here!" his voice called urgently on the heels of the report.

She hurried in response. He was kneeling by yet another window. "What?" she gasped, dropping to her knees beside him.

"Look there!" He pointed through the shattered glass.

Barbara sucked in her breath sharply as she saw the smoke and the first flickering flames rising from the chick coop. The fowls had long since scattered.

"They torched it!" Pete cried bitterly. "I couldn't get the one who did it." Despair sounded in his voice, and Barbara felt it twist in her heart.

"Well?" Rathers sang out arrogantly. "What'll it be? You got about a minute to make up your minds! Then I torch the house!"

Chapter Thirteen

For long minutes Glen crouched beside the mouth of the cave. It wasn't much wider than his shoulders, and he would have to dip his head to enter. He held the vines back just enough to let him get a look inside, but the blackness there defeated his vision.

At last he tossed a stone inside and heard it rattle and clatter away into silence. Nothing responded. Conscious of the passage of time, he rigged a crude torch and lit a match to it. Then, torch gripped in his left fist and revolver leveled in his right, he ducked through the vine doorway and into the cave.

The floor slanted downward at a slight angle. The flame of the torch shone on naked stone. After only a few steps he could walk upright. He knew the torch made him a dandy target for any enemy lurking ahead of him, but he was not about to proceed blind into this hole.

On the seventh step he felt the tug of a cord against his ankle. Instinctively he twisted aside, accidentally slamming the butt of the slung Sporting Rifle against the wall as he turned. He heard a twanging sound and a whisper of air as something streaked past him. It glanced from an outthrusting bulge in the wall and fell just within the cave mouth. Glen saw that it was an arrow.

He found the bow rigged to the tripline a little farther along. It was crudely made, but looked to be powerful. Nothing real fancy, he mused, but the booby trap was more than capable of skewering an unsuspecting intruder.

Warily he edged on deeper into the cave, alert for more pitfalls. But none presented themselves, and he emerged at length into a widening of the passage. Glen paused and eyed the chamber in the uncertain light of the torch.

A rough-hewn chair and table served as the furnishings. Against one wall was a pallet of leaves and rags. A rat scurried away in the darkness. Offal and scraps of rotting food littered the floor. Glen's nostrils flared at the foul odor. More than anything else, the place reminded him of the den of some near-human beast.

A gleam of metal in the far corner caught his eye. Curious, he advanced a couple of paces, then froze rigid. His hand tightened reflexively on the Colt in his fist.

A human skull, encased in metal, grinned evilly at him from a metallic corpse. It took Glen a moment to understand he was staring at a skeleton still clad in an ancient suit of pitted Spanish armor. The rusty length of a sword lay beside the sepulchral figure. Glen saw that the sword hilt was nestled amid the small pile of bones that had once been fingers. Whoever the dead man had been, he had died clutching his sword.

Swallowing hard, Glen went to stand over the eerie figure. In the light of the torch the skull seemed to wink at him with arcane secret knowledge.

Glen had heard the tales of the old Spanish conquistadors who had penetrated these mountains in their tireless searching for gold and glory. Often they had clashed with the Indian tribes inhabiting the mountains in those ancient days. Here lay one of that hardy breed. Wounded, perhaps, this worthy had dragged himself to sanctuary and died alone, ready to meet his enemy until the last. His sanctuary had become his tomb, and here he had lain for centuries.

Glen shivered and looked involuntarily about him. Only Quirt, he reflected darkly, would leave this forgotten corpse here to share his foul den with him.

Suddenly Glen was anxious to be gone from this haunted place. He reset the bow and then erased all traces of his presence. Let Quirt remain ignorant of his knowledge of its existence.

A small tunnel continued from the chamber. Guessing Quirt wouldn't let himself be hemmed into a trap with only one way out, Glen followed it. He had to bend almost double in some places, and twist sideways to accommodate the bulky length of the rifle on his back. At last, he climbed and scrambled up into daylight, emerging in a thicket of brush atop a rocky knoll.

Quirt must return to his den eventually, he calculated. If he could find a vantage point that gave him a clear field of fire on both entrances to the cave, he just might be able to feed the bushwhacker a lead taste of his own ugly medicine.

Careful to stay under cover, he employed his field glasses to scan the surrounding geography. He settled on a barren ridge about a quarter mile distant that looked to give him the placement he wanted.

By the time he reached it and clambered up among its rocky outcroppings, the sun was well overhead. He could feel the stones about him absorbing the heat as he settled in behind a natural bulwark. In moments he was sweating, and he took a moment to swig water from his canteen.

He checked the scope on the Sporting Rifle and used it to peer in turn at both entryways to the cave. Satisfied with his line of fire, he jacked a shell into the chamber, set his field glasses and canteen to hand, and settled down to wait.

The sun began to cook him. He felt its heat eating

into him through the fabric of his shirt. Far overhead he saw the notch-winged silhouette of a vulture drifting in the still air. The bones of men and monsters littered these mountains. He hoped his own wouldn't join them.

It became hard to keep his attention on the two target points below him. The unrelenting pressure of the heat and the ceaseless strain stretching his nerves taut combined to weigh burdensomely on him. Yet he stayed as still as possible, conscious that a trained eye could detect movement at a great distance.

The sun passed its height and began to slide slowly down the pale western sky. Glen amused himself by wondering what Quirt was up to. Was he likewise situated someplace, waiting for Glen to appear in the sights of his Sharps?

Sweat trickled into the corner of Glen's eye. He blinked it away, then squeezed his eyelids shut to relieve the strain from squinting the glare.

When he opened his eyes, he saw Quirt.

The bounty man was just a dimly glimpsed form slinking through the brush and rocks toward the main entrance to his lair. Glen breathed in and exhaled softly. With extreme care, making no sudden movements, he eased the Sporting Rifle up into position and shifted his legs under him into a sniper's kneeling stance.

Through the scope sight Quirt sprang into view. He carried his Sharps in one hand, and his gliding movements put Glen to mind of a lean, tawny puma.

Intervening growth and boulders prevented a sure shot. Glen waited, sure that Quirt would pause instinctively before actually entering his den through the curtain of vines.

Once more sweat blurred his vision. Carefully he lowered his head and used his fingertips to flick the moisture away. Then he sighted through the scope and down the long octagonal barrel.

Revulsion rose suddenly in him at what he was fixing to do. Never before had he fired on a man without giving him a chance to surrender. In the same way Quirt must've knelt and drawn a head on each of his victims. But they had been innocents. Quirt was a cold-blooded killer who, given the chance, might turn the tables on Glen in an instant. He was deserving of no more mercy than he'd given his own victims.

Glen's finger curled firmly around the trigger. He forced his muscles to relax. At the mouth of his den, Quirt halted like a wild beast. Glen imagined him testing the air with his nostrils for traces of any intruder. Glen squeezed the trigger.

As he fired, Quirt moved. Warned by a sixth sense, or some betraying sign of his presence, Glen didn't know. But Quirt ducked and dodged, then turned and vanished into the brush as the big rifle's echoes slammed back and forth between the mountain peaks.

Glen hurtled the outcropping that had sheltered him and went plunging down the ridge in pursuit. He didn't know if he had hit Quirt. In the feverish moment of the chase it didn't matter. He had been too close, too near to finishing this, to let Quirt evade him now.

At first his stiffened legs almost betrayed him, but his downward momentum kept him moving until he got his feet properly under him. He didn't think a rockslide could've gone down the grade much faster.

A bullet struck rock somewhere nearby and ricocheted off with a scream as he reached the bottom of the grade. He sensed that it hadn't been aimed so much as it had been fired back in his direction to discourage pursuit. He flung himself to cover just the same, then began to work his way forward.

He gained a stand of pine partway up a steep hogback, then paused to listen and catch his breath. A shot echoed. The boom of the Sharps was plainly identifiable. Glen couldn't tell where the bullet went, but he felt a grim satisfaction. Rattled, Quirt was firing blind, throwing an occasional slug behind him to slow his pursuer down. Glen had the bushwhacker on the run.

He pressed on toward the source of the shot. The echoes made it tricky, but he'd heard and done enough shooting in these mountains so that he could put a pretty good guess as to the shooter's whereabouts.

A crimson smear caught his eye. Blood marked the stone at the edge of a thicket. Broken branches showed where Quirt had simply bulled his way through like a man fleeing wildly. More blood showed on a stickery limb. Wounded, Quirt might be an even greater menace, but Glen would be a fool not to press him hard, now that he was hurt.

He followed Quirt's pathway into the dense brush, using the rifle at times to probe ahead of him. He felt its barrel strike a limb, which collapsed. Something shining and metallic whiplashed out at his thigh. He lurched back, and saw he'd come awful close to blundering into a simple booby trap. Quirt's bowie knife was affixed to a flexible limb that had been pulled back and propped in place by a piece of forked wood that served as a trigger. If his foot, and not his gun, had hit the trigger, the bowie would've transfixed his thigh.

Sobered, he moved on more warily, keeping his eyes peeled for any other nasty surprises Quirt might've rigged. The blood splotches continued to lure him. They appeared with greater frequency now, although, taken in total, they didn't add up to much real blood loss. Still, Glen reckoned, the wound had to have reduced his quarry's speed to some extent.

The afternoon was slipping past. Glen increased his pace, emerging at last onto a wide ledge overlooking a barren gorge. He paused, baffled. The gap was almost eleven hundred yards wide. The far side of the gorge was at a higher elevation than the ledge where he stood. A steep grade ascended behind it. Quirt had disappeared.

The shot from across the gorge seared stone beside him. He dived for the cover of a pile of boulders as another shot followed the first by not much more than a clocktick's time. He flattened himself behind the boulder, and realization of how he'd been hoodwinked swept over him.

If Quirt had really been wounded, he could never have gotten far enough ahead to cross the gorge and take up the sniper's position he now held. But cross it he had, no doubt using secret trails known only to him and the mountain goats.

The blood spots had been a sham, Glen understood. Quirt must've deliberately cut himself and left a trail to draw Glen on. The booby trap with the knife was meant only to buy time. Quirt would never seriously have expected a manhunter of Glen's experience to fall for it. But it slowed him down, made him look for other snares, and it had given Quirt time to reach his vantage point on the opposite side of the gorge. He had lain in wait, almost as he had done when Glen had stalked him on the first disastrous occasion.

A third shot came hard on the heels of the second. Only an expert could fire a single-shot Sharps that fast. Glen knew how Quirt was doing it. He had placed three of the .50-caliber shells between the fingers of his left hand. Then, as he fired, he was able to lever open the breech and deftly pluck another shell and slide it into place. Glen glimpsed the powdersmoke hanging over a brush-studded outcropping as a fourth shot whined past his ear. He was awful close to becoming Quirt's victim once again.

But things were a mite different than they'd been the first time. Glen surged up on one knee, raising the big Winchester smoothly to his shoulder. Rapid-fire, slamming the lever and pulling the trigger so fast his movements were a blur, he pumped all eight 50-110 shells from the Sporting Rifle into the distant outcropping. And Quirt, unexpectedly confronted with more concentrated firepower than he'd likely ever faced, probably more than he'd even known existed, broke from cover and went scrabbling up the steep grade toward a higher elevation. From there, his Sharps still might give him an edge.

Frantically Glen jammed more cartridges into the magazine. He rose to his feet and stepped into the clear, sighting at that distant scrambling figure. Without the scope sight, it would've been about like aiming at a fly. He cut loose, and sensed that he had missed, the shot going low.

But it came close enough to unnerve Quirt once more. He reached a level spot and halted, wheeling as he lifted the Sharps. Like Glen, he was in plain view, out in the open, and he was sighting through his scope across nearly twelve hundred yards of distance—almost a mile.

Marksmen's duel. It seemed to Glen he could look right down the yawning barrel of the Sharps. He felt the kick of the Sporting Rifle at the same instant he saw smoke puff from Quirt's gun.

A miniature cannonball tore past Glen's ear a second later. Through the haze of powdersmoke he glimpsed Quirt's tiny figure spin about and fall. He followed the tumbling form till it came to rest on the ledge below. The Sharps slid to a halt a few feet away.

Glen lowered the Sporting Rifle. Echoes bounced and reverberated his skull. His arms went suddenly weak, and he had to let the Winchester sag to his waist.

He plodded to the edge of the gorge. There had to be a way down, he told himself, over to the opposite side.

It took him an hour of climbing and hiking and struggling over rocks before he stood at last at the foot of the grade on the far side of the gorge.

Amazingly, Quirt still lived. He lay near his Sharps, which had been busted in the fall, and stared up at Glen with dimming eyes. "What'd you use on me, Deputy?" he rasped.

Glen hefted the Winchester. "Repeater," he said.

Quirt focused blearily on the rifle. "Ain't ever seen one that big," he said in awe.

"You have now."

"Never would've gotten me without it," Quirt boasted, and died.

"Probably not," Glen told him anyway.

Chapter Fourteen

The lonely braying of a mule led Glen to a nearby box canyon early the next morning. A crude fence had been erected across its mouth. The mule itself was gaunt and spooky of strangers, but it settled down quickly enough when he put a rope on it. With much snorting and eye-rolling, it submitted to having Quirt's tarp-wrapped body tied to its back. Glen roped the busted Sharps to its owner. Again astride the pinto, he headed down out of the Arbuckles, leading the mule and its grisly burden.

Once back on the prairie, he started toward his place. The day was waning, but he wanted to clean up before he toted the body into town for the Citizens Committee. There was still nothing to link Quirt directly to Rathers, he brooded as he rode. For that matter, it would be difficult to prove conclusively that Quirt had been the bushwhacker. But, Glen mused wrly, he was willing to bet that the killings stopped.

When he saw the smoke against the late afternoon sky, he stiffened with a plainsman's automatic apprehension of a prairie fire. Then the distant popping of shots came to him, and, with it, a notion of what might be the source of the smoke.

He unslipped the lead rope and put heels hard to the pinto, leaving the mule staring curiously after him. Delivery of the dead bushwhacker would have to wait. He had a nasty hunch that Rathers had taken matters into his own hands at last.

The pinto stretched out, and Glen bent low in the saddle. The horse's muscles surged and flowed beneath him. He felt the wind of their passage in his face.

The Turner homestead came into view. Flames were licking up from one of the outbuildings. A surge of relief went through Glen. The house was still intact, although horsemen galloped about and gunfire flamed between them and the house. There was stiff resistance, and Glen didn't doubt that the house would be the next structure to taste the torch.

With the pinto at a dead run, he unshipped the massive length of the Sporting Rifle and hoisted it to his shoulder. He didn't expect to hit much from horseback, but maybe he could get their attention. He sighted down the long barrel as best he could and pulled the trigger.

It was a mistake. The recoil of the rifle slammed his shoulder and almost spun him out of the saddle. Unused to its cannon's blast, the pinto swerved wildly. Glen clamped his legs tight about the body of the horse and hauled back hard on the reins. The pinto's haunches dropped, and he skidded to a halt. Glen kicked free of the stirrups and hit the ground with rifle in hand.

One of the attackers seemed to have heard the shot. He had reined in his horse and was gazing hard in Glen's direction. Five hundred yards, Glen estimated automatically. He had removed the scope, and didn't figure on taking time to replace it now.

He drew a bead on the rider, then cut loose the thunder. The fellow had just started to wheel his mount when he went sprawling out of the saddle. His horse bolted. Glen jacked the rifle lever without lowering the weapon and shifted aim to another rider. Briefly he tracked his target, led it by just a little, and fired again. The gunman toppled sideward. Riderless, his horse raced on.

Now Glen had their attention. Two of their number had gone down, and one man was rallying them to this new threat. Glen fired once more and missed. His target spurred his horse and took off without looking back. Glen let him go; he was no longer a danger.

But the ringleader had succeeded in marshaling his forces. Glen heard a faint rebel yell, and a half dozen horsemen, guns blazing, came at him in a ragged charge.

The terrain was flat out; no place to run or take cover. Glen stood where he was, coolly thumbing more shells into the magazine. He lifted the big Sporting Rifle like a soldier on the firing range, as the bullets began to snap past him.

Deliberately he set his sights on the center rider—the closest—and dropped the hammer. The hired gun went backward off his horse as if he'd been yanked by a lariat. They were a hundred yards closer to him; five of them were left. Glen lined the octagonal barrel on the next man, sighted through the smoke, and let the thunder of the heavy repeater roll across the prairie once more. His target somersaulted backward and was lost to sight. His horse sheared off in front of another beast, spooking it. The rider fought it under control, then spun it about and hightailed it back the way he had come.

Glen was wreathed in powdersmoke. He stepped clear of it and fired again—a miss. The remaining three riders were closing fast, zigzagging their mounts to make more difficult targets. It worked. Glen had to use two more shots before another attacker was swatted from his horse.

He had three bullets left, and the final two riders were a hundred yards out. Glen fired and came close enough to make one of the attackers jerk his horse hard to the side. Glen knocked him out of the saddle with his next shot.

But the final horseman was still coming, and he was

firing his six-gun with a deliberate steady coolness. Glen saw that it was the ramrod, Reno.

Glen waved the smoke away and lined the Sporting Rifle. Reno must've seen his action; he ducked just as Glen made his shot. The bullet went high. Reno gave a savage victory yell as he saw Glen let the empty rifle sag to his side in his left hand.

"Blast you, Douglas! You shot my whole crew to pieces!" the ramrod shouted. He came in like a cavalry officer leading a charge, pistol spitting flame.

Glen shot him too. He snapped his Colt up and clear of leather in a single deft movement of arm and wrist. He glimpsed the shocked look on Reno's weather-beaten face a half instant before he put a bullet squarely through the ramrod's shoulder. Reno's gun fell away beneath his mount's hooves. With its rider slumping in the saddle, the horse rocked to a stop twenty-five feet short of where Glen stood.

Glen dashed forward and caught Reno as he slid from the saddle. The segundo grunted in pain as Glen let him collapse to the ground.

"Rathers is behind the bushwhackings, isn't he?" Glen demanded savegly. Now, at last, he could get the truth about this ugly business.

"Yeah," Reno gasped. "He hired that loco dry-gulcher. Sent me up in the mountains to pay him and keep him in tobacco and whiskey and bullets."

"Why?" Glen jabbed the barrel of his revolver down toward Reno's face. "What did he hope to gain?"

"Lay off!" Reno panted. "I'll tell you! I've had my bellyful of Rathers and his crazy schemes."

"Talk!" Glen snapped.

Reno swallowed, shivering with the shock of his wound. "Some bigwig up in Washington told him that when this Territory is opened for settlement, anybody leasing Indian land automatically gets legal ownership of whatever he's leasing, no matter how many acres it is. I don't know if that's true, but Rathers believed it. He's as hungry for land as a starving hound is for a bone!" Reno broke off with a grimace. "By heaven, Douglas, I need a doctor!"

"You waited mighty late to start calling on heaven," Glen growled. "But I'll see you get to a sawbones. Wouldn't want you dying on me. Judge Parker will be awful interested in hearing what you have to say."

"Anything, Douglas! Just don't let me lie here and bleed to death!"

There wasn't much risk of that, but Glen didn't tell him so. "Where is Rathers now?" he prodded.

"Back there at the Turner place, last I saw. He rode with us. Must be lying low, the yellow dog!"

Glen snapped his head up to look toward the ranch buildings. Pete and Barbara could still be in danger.

Even as he looked, he saw the mounted form of the ranch owner, recognizable even at a distance, break from around the corner of the house in a mad dash for safety. As he went by the porch, a sturdy figure burst from the doorway and flung himself from the porch in a straining dive. In midair Pete Turner crashed into Rathers, and they plunged out of the saddle in a flurry of arms and booted feet.

Glen ran for the pinto. Reno was in no shape to go anywhere; he would keep. But right now Pete might have his hands full.

A cloud of dust obscured the combatants as Glen raced the pinto into the yard. But as he made a flying dismount the dust cleared to show Pete, one fist drawn back, lifting a sagging Rather from the ground by his shirtfront. Barbara was on the porch. Glen's rifle was gripped in her white-knuckled hands.

"No, Pete!" she cried. "He's had enough!"

"She's right," Glen said. "Leave something for Judge Parker."

Grudgingly Pete let the battered rancher slump flat to the ground. Pete wore a few bruises himself, but there was a new rugged assurance to his movements as he backed away a couple of steps.

"We held them off," he told Glen between panting breaths.

"I reckon you did," Glen acknowledged. Rathers, he noted, had lost his pearl-handled revolver in the struggle.

Barbara set the rifle aside and flew down the steps to Glen. Automatically he put an arm around her shoulders and pulled her against his side. It felt right having her there.

"You got nothing on me, Douglas!" Rathers blustered, propping himself up on one elbow. He touched his bleeding lip and winced.

"Reno will spill his guts, given a choice between that or the noose," Glen predicted coldly. "He can tie you to the drygulchings."

"That don't mean anything!" Rathers stormed. "Some madman has been doing those killings."

"You might be right about that," Glen conceded, "but you were paying him to do it."

"You'll have to catch him to prove anything."

Glen jerked his head back over his shoulder. "I got his carcass tied over his own mule out on the prairie."

Rathers glared at him in shock. "Nobody could bring Quirt in!" he protested vehemently. "How'd you do it?"

"Bushwhacked him."

"They were fixing to burn us out!" Pete put in.

Glen glanced at the smoldering remains of the chicken coop. There was no danger of the flames spreading. The small structure had burned to the ground. All that was left was a pile of smoldering debris. He cast his eyes on about, noting for the first time the body of a man sprawled in the dust. Near the corral, a saddled horse limped awkwardly. Pete was right in saying they'd held off the attackers, he mused. Ranger prowled warily.

Barbara stirred at his side and looked up at him with anxious eyes. "Are you all right, Glen? I was so worried."

"I'm fine," Glen assured her.

The bushwhacker—the man who killed Dad . . .''
she began in a questioning tone.

"He's dead, just like I told Rathers." Glen felt her
shudder beside him.

"Back there, behind the house," she said softly, "I
think I killed a man."

"If you hadn't, they would've killed you and your
brother."

Rathers shifted on the ground, his muscles tensing.
Pete saw it at the same moment as Glen. The youth
moved swiftly, mounting the steps to the porch and
snatching up the rifle Barbara had left there. He was
down the steps in a bound, covering the fallen rancher.

"Don't move!" he snapped. "You got a lot to answer for, including the killing of my pa!"

"He'll answer for it all," Glen said.

There were a lot of things left to do, he reflected.
But, for the moment, with victory finally his, it was
good to stand with Barbara at his side. She would
make a better wife than he could've ever asked for,
and Pete would make a fine brother-in-law.

Glen felt the weight in his left hand. He glanced
down and saw the Sporting Rifle still in his grip. He
realized he'd kept it in hand ever since the gunfight
on the prairie when it had stood him in such good
stead.

He smiled a little ruefully. He didn't figure he'd be
needing his bushwhacker's gun anymore.